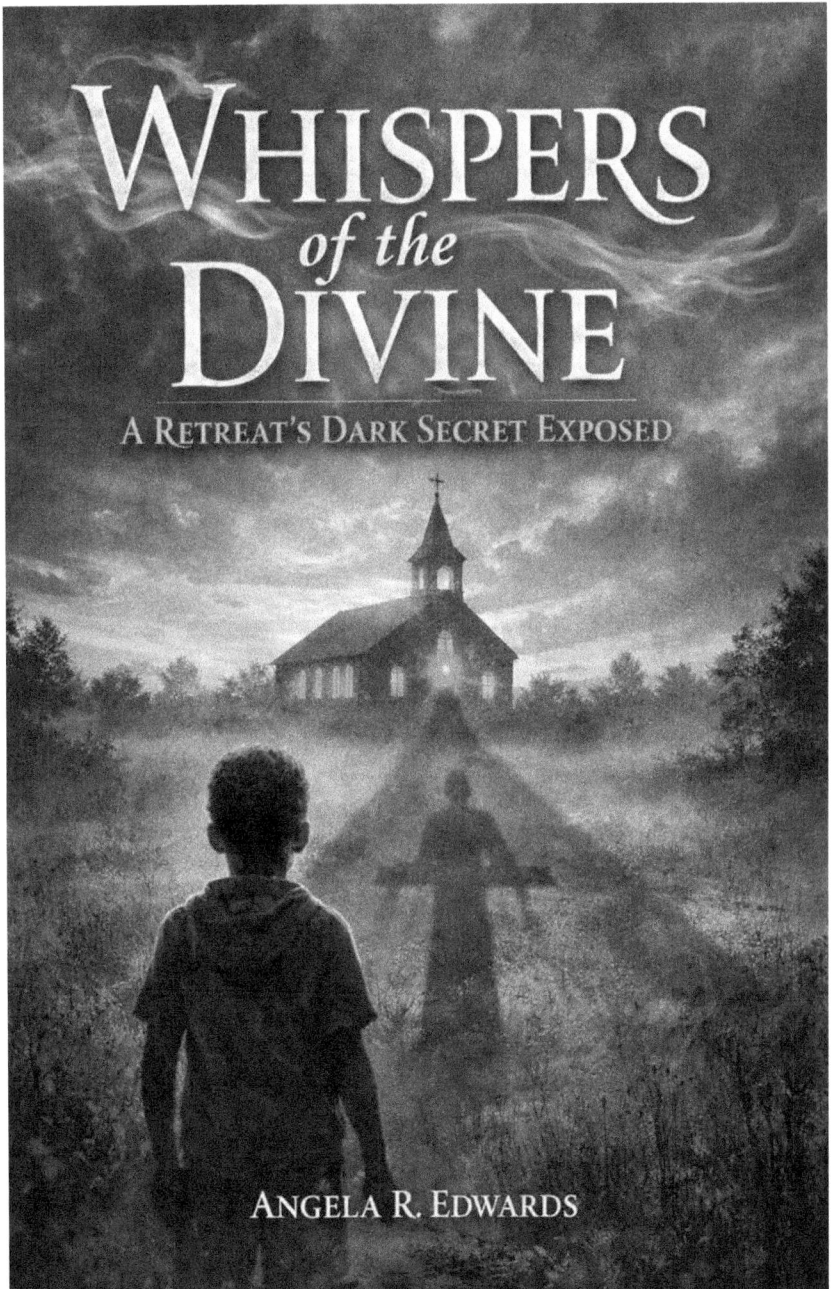

WHISPERS OF THE

DIVINE

A Retreat's Dark Secret Exposed

Angela R. Edwards

Pearly Gates Publishing LLC
INSPIRING CHRISTIAN AUTHORS TO BE AUTHORS

Pearly Gates Publishing, LLC, Harlem, GA (USA)

Whispers of the Divine:
A Retreat's Dark Secret Exposed

Scripture references are used with permission via Zondervan at Biblegateway.com. Public Domain.

Hardcover ISBN 13: 979-8-276954-74-5
Independently Published
Paperback ISBN 13: 978-1-948853-88-0
Library of Congress Control Number: 2025942816
First Edition: April 6, 2026

For information and bulk ordering, contact:
Pearly Gates Publishing, LLC
Angela Edwards, Chief Editorial Director
P.O. Box 639
Harlem, GA 30814
pearlygatespublishing@gmail.com

Dedication

To every soul carrying the invisible scars of church hurt, this is for you. For those who have felt the sting of a sanctuary turning bitter, may these words serve as a gentle reminder that God's love exceeds human flaws. Your wounds are seen, and your journey is honored. The Divine still whispers your name with tenderness, waiting patiently beyond the shadows of disappointment for your heart's return. When human hands fail to reflect divine love, remember that God has never left your side. May these words create a soothing space in your soul where healing begins, and faith discovers new roots—not in perfect institutions, but in God's perfect love that never abandons.

Preface

Faith has always been my anchor, but like any relationship of substance, my journey with the church has weathered seasons of profound disillusionment alongside moments of transcendent grace. Writing *Whispers of the Divine* emerged from this complex terrain—the sacred space where doubt and devotion coexist, where institutional failure meets personal resilience.

I still remember that Sunday morning when whispers flowed through our congregation like an unseen current. I was just a teen then, but I sensed something was amiss. Our pastor, a man whose sermons on family values had guided us for many years, was not at the pulpit. In his place, the associate pastor delivered a vague message about "praying for church leadership," but the truth had already slipped out through quiet conversations in the sanctuary. The pastor had been accused of having an affair with a church member. Even more shocking was the revelation that he had fathered a child, whom he had secretly supported while publicly denying any wrongdoing.

As a devoted member who had entrusted my spiritual development to this man's guidance, I sensed something fundamentally break within me. This wasn't just disappointment in a fallen leader; it was a betrayal that questioned every sermon on integrity he preached, every prayer I had whispered alongside a man I barely recognized.

The church board's initial response only worsened the wound. There were carefully crafted statements about "alleged indiscretions" and calls for forgiveness before the whole truth was even acknowledged. When the evidence became undeniable, some suggested that the entire matter be handled "within the family of God"—code for protecting both the pastor and the institution from public scrutiny.

That experience planted the first seeds of what would eventually become this novel. I began questioning not just individual failings but the systems that protect power at the expense of truth.

Several years later, at a different church in a new state, where I was looking for fresh ground for my wounded faith, I experienced another moment of institutional disillusionment that was even more personal. My son and one of his friends kept having conflicts with another child in the neighborhood, which was probably common for teenagers, but it had escalated to a screaming match and violence involving a weapon (a loaded BB gun, to be exact) at my home.

Following the biblical model for conflict resolution outlined in Matthew 18:15-20, I requested a private meeting with the pastor and the assailant's mother after my direct conversations with the parents failed to produce a resolution.

I will never forget sitting in the pastor's office, vulnerability raw in my voice as I shared my son's pain, only to watch his expression shift from pastoral concern to political calculation when he learned whose child was involved—the son of an influential member, a family whose name was well-known throughout the church community. Suddenly, my legitimate concern became a complex problem to manage.

"Sometimes, teenagers misinterpret things," he explained, his tone dripping with patronizing reassurance. "I know this family well, and I'm certain there's been a misunderstanding. Perhaps your son is being a bit sensitive?"

(Those weren't his exact words, but that was the gist of where the blame was placed... on my child.)

My son's and my concerns were dismissed while church politics prevailed. The message couldn't have been clearer: some families mattered more than others. Some voices carried weight while others remained whispers.

Those experiences forced me to confront difficult questions: Can we separate faith from its institutions? How do we remain faithful when those entrusted with spiritual authority prove unworthy of that trust? What happens when the structures designed to nurture our souls cause harm instead?

Whispers of the Divine emerged from this wrestling in my spirit. Through the fictional community of First Community Church and the journeys of Pastor James Miller, Rebecca Chen, and young Michael, I've explored how truth eventually surfaces despite our human efforts to bury it. This story acknowledges the very real pain caused by religious hypocrisy while affirming that authentic faith can survive—even thrive—after institutional betrayal.

My personal journey has taught me that questioning is not the enemy of faith but its necessary companion. That disillusionment, painful as it is, often clears the way for something more genuine to emerge: God's voice continuing to speak even when human channels have proven flawed.

If you've ever felt the sting of betrayal by those claiming spiritual authority, questioned whether faith can survive institutional failure, or wondered how truth can eventually pierce through layers of deception, this story is for you.

May *Whispers of the Divine* offer honest recognition of "church hurt" and hope for faith refined—not charred beyond recognition—by fire.

Introduction

In the quietest moments, when the noise of life dies down and we are alone with our thoughts, many of us hear them... **whispers**. Not loud voices, but persistent questions that come from deep inside us.

Is faith still possible in a world where religious institutions fail so spectacularly?

Can communities recover from profound betrayal?

Is pursuing the truth worth the high cost?

These whispers grow louder during times of crisis—when headlines expose corruption in sacred spaces, when trusted leaders fall, and when systems meant to protect actually cause harm. They become discordant when crises hit us personally, when our communities face their darkest moments, and when faith itself seems at risk due to human failure.

Pastor James Miller has heard these whispers throughout his life, both personally and professionally. As a pastor who previously served in law enforcement, he has witnessed the damage caused when power supplants service, when image supersedes substance, and when institutions prioritize protecting themselves over those they serve. He has sat with victims whose trust was broken not just by individual betrayals, but also by systemic failures. He counseled congregations shaken by revelations when their spiritual home hid darkness alongside light.

Yet he has also witnessed something else—something remarkable that happens when communities choose to face brutal truths instead of hiding from them. He has seen healing arise from acknowledgment, strength emerge from vulnerability, and authentic faith ignite from the ashes of religious pretense.

It is this paradoxical journey—from devastation to restoration, from whispers of doubt to declarations of renewed purpose—that lies at the heart of this book.

The story that unfolds on these pages examines a territory many would rather avoid. It addresses the uncomfortable truth that some religious institutions, despite their lofty ideals and sacred purposes, are still vulnerable to the same corrupting influences that affect "all" human organizations. Power can intoxicate those in spiritual authority. Financial temptations don't fade behind stained glass windows. Self-protective instincts sometimes override theological commitments to truth and transparency.

But alas, this is not primarily a cautionary tale about institutional failure. Instead, it explores how authentic faith endures—dare I say even **thrives**—when it's freed from false certainties and comfortable illusions. It invites us to consider whether true spiritual transformation may actually involve confronting the failures we most fear exposing.

Throughout human history, religious communities have faced moments of existential crises. Scandals have threatened their core stories. Betrayals have eroded moral authority. Failures have contradicted their stated values. Some communities respond by shutting down, denying problems, silencing critics, and ultimately protecting their institutions at the expense of integrity.

Others choose a different path. They admit mistakes, take meaningful action to change, make room for sorrow alongside hope, and find that truth—no matter how painful at first—eventually leads to liberation.

The fictional community presented here stands at a crucial crossroads. At first glance, First Community Church appears to represent the best of religious traditions: steady leadership, active programs, and a respected position within its broader community. However, beneath this polished exterior lies a hidden network of secrets spanning decades—a conspiracy of silence that has undermined the very foundation necessary for genuine faith.

When these secrets start to surface—spurred by an eight-year-old boy's innocent discovery during a spiritual retreat—the congregation faces questions that go beyond their specific situation. How can a community rebuild trust once it has been broken? What sets healthy authority apart from abusive power? Can institutions establish safeguards against corruption without becoming so rigid that they lose their spiritual core?

Most fundamentally: Is God present during the painful process of exposing and reckoning, or only in the comfort of certainty and stability?

These questions reach far beyond church walls. In an era when trust in institutions has declined sharply across various sectors—ranging from government to healthcare, from education to media—many wonder if communal structures can still endure. Some turn inward, concluding that personal spirituality means abandoning organized religion altogether. Others hold tighter to authority figures who promise certainty amid chaos, sacrificing critical thinking for the comfort of clear guidance. Between these extremes lies a linear path—one that neither forsakes community nor dismisses discernment—valuing both tradition and change, and recognizing that institutions are both flawed and essential.

It is this middle path—complex and uncertain, yet ultimately life-affirming—that *Whispers of the Divine* explores through its unfolding story. The characters you will encounter represent diverse reactions to institutional failure.

Rebecca Chen, a mother whose child becomes entangled in church corruption, faces the spiritual vertigo of questioning a community that previously offered her comfort after a personal tragedy.

Detective Sarah Collins approaches her work with professional skepticism, shaped by her past experiences with religious hypocrisy, but remains open to genuine faith when she sees it.

Eleanor Simmons embodies the paradoxical strength of the overlooked and underestimated—an elderly church secretary whose patient documentation over 15 years ultimately reveals what powerful men worked desperately to hide.

At the center is Pastor James Miller, whose dual background in law enforcement and ministry creates both internal conflict and a unique perspective as he navigates the tension between justice, mercy, his responsibility to a traumatized congregation, and his obligation to truth, regardless of the consequences. Through his journey, we see how spiritual leadership changes when stripped of positional authority and institutional protection.

Come. Lean in close, and listen carefully for the *Whispers of the Divine*...

Table of Contents

Chapter 1: Sacred Grounds

The winding mountain road seemed to refresh Pastor James Miller's spirit with each twist and turn. As his aging SUV climbed higher into the Appalachian foothills, the chaotic cityscape faded away, replaced by thick forests of oak and pine that stood like ancient guardians. James rolled down his window, letting the cool September air fill his lungs. The smell of earth and pine needles replaced the lingering aroma of the three-hour-old coffee in his cup holder.

For 50 years, Mount Hermon Retreat Center had been a sanctuary for many Christian congregants, a place where Heaven felt almost within reach. The final bend in the road revealed the retreat grounds—a clearing nestled in a natural amphitheater of mountains, as if God Himself had cupped His hands to create a space set apart from the rest of the world.

James parked his vehicle at the main lodge and stepped out, his boots crunching on the gravel. The main building was an impressive structure of timber and stone, with a vaulted ceiling that reached toward the sky and walls of windows that welcomed the surrounding mountains. A carved wooden cross, weathered by decades of mountain seasons, stood tall beside the entrance. *"Lord, let this be a weekend of renewal. Not just for them, but for me, too,"* he prayed silently.

"Pastor Miller! You beat us here." Eleanor Simmons waved from her old blue Buick that had just pulled up. At 72, the church secretary moved with surprising agility, her silver hair shining in the morning sunlight as she hurried toward him.

"Eleanor, I asked you to call me James," he replied, embracing the woman who had served First Community Church since before he was born.

"And I've told you I'll do no such thing," she said with the comfortable stubbornness of a long friendship. "I have respect for the position, even if the man in it is younger than my favorite cardigan."

James smiled, but it didn't quite reach his eyes. Eleanor had known him since he was a young boy sitting in the back pew with restless legs. She'd witnessed his journey from a troubled teen to a police officer, then his sudden career change after the Henderson case that still haunted his dreams. She'd been there when he answered the call to ministry, when he married Rebecca, and when he buried her seven years later.

"Youth Pastor Parker just called," Eleanor said, mercifully interrupting his thoughts. "They're 30 minutes out with the kids. The bus is apparently experiencing the joy of what Ethan called 'spiritual singing,' but what I suspect is more akin to cheerful chaos."

"My God. Twenty children under 12 at a mountain retreat. What could possibly go wrong?" James chuckled as he lifted Eleanor's bag from her car.

"The Lord works in mysterious ways, Pastor. Sometimes, those ways involve children's sticky fingers on freshly painted walls."

They approached the main building, where Deacon Thomas Webb was directing the weekend staff on final preparations. Thomas' imposing frame and booming voice commanded attention; his silver-streaked dark hair remained perfectly in place despite the brisk mountain breeze. "James! There you are." Thomas stepped forward, clipboard in hand.

"We've got the chapel ready, dining hall stocked, and cabins prepared. Just waiting on the final assignment list from you."

James nodded, pulling out a folded paper from his pocket. "Four children per cabin. Eleanor and Rebecca Chen will supervise the girls. Ethan and I will handle the boys. Are you sure you don't mind managing logistics from the main lodge?"

"My retreating days are behind me," Thomas said with a tight smile. "These old bones prefer a proper mattress. Besides, someone needs to coordinate with the kitchen staff and handle any... let's call them 'issues' that may arise," he replied hesitantly.

There was something in Thomas' tone that caught James' attention—a subtle tension that seemed at odds with the man's usual confidence. Before he could inquire, the retreat center's caretaker, Martin Grayson, approached with practical questions about the weekend schedule. As they finalized details, James' thoughts drifted to the families that would soon arrive. This weekend was meant to strengthen faith and community, particularly important for the newer members like Rebecca Chen and her son, Michael. Following her husband's death two years ago, Rebecca had found her way to First Community Church, seeking answers and solace. Her son Michael, bright-eyed and inquisitive, had quickly become a favorite in Sunday School.

The sound of tires rolling on the gravel announced new arrivals. Rebecca's modest sedan pulled into the parking area. She stepped out with a warm smile that masked the grief she still carried. At 34, she had a quiet strength and sincere faith that humbled James. "Pastor James! So good to see you again!"

Michael leaped out of the backseat, his eight-year-old energy impossible to contain. "We found a turtle on the road, but mom made me leave it there—even though I promised to bring it back Sunday," he announced as he hurried toward James.

"The retreat center probably has enough wildlife without your contribution this time," James said, laughing as he ruffled the boy's dark hair.

"But I named it already. Shelly!" The laughter in his eyes betrayed Michael's earnest disappointment.

Rebecca approached more calmly, carrying two modest duffel bags. "I apologize for his enthusiasm. It's been 'turtle this' and 'turtle that' for the last 20 miles."

"Enthusiasm is why we're here," James replied, taking the bags from her. "Faith without excitement is just a habit."

"Wise words, Pastor," Rebecca said with a gentle smile. "Michael has been counting down the days. This is our first retreat with the church."

"And we're glad to have you both," he replied sincerely. The Chen family embodied exactly what he hoped this retreat would foster: genuine faith in the midst of life's toughest challenges. As they headed toward the registration table, Michael skipped ahead, seemingly having already forgotten Shelly the turtle in favor of exploring his new surroundings. "He seems to be adjusting well," James observed carefully.

Rebecca's expression softened with maternal pride. "Children are resilient. Some days are harder than others, but his counselor says he's processing David's death in healthy ways." She paused. "This place feels special. Like it's set apart somehow."

"That's exactly what the founders intended," James confirmed. "Mount Hermon is named after the mountain in the Bible where the transfiguration occurred—where the divine broke through into the ordinary. Three of the New Testament Gospels—Matthew, Mark, and Luke—speak of a 'high mountain.'"

The sound of a bus engine interrupted their conversation. Around the bend, the church's white bus appeared, decorated with colorful handprints and the church logo. It parked with a hiss of brakes, and moments later, the doors opened, releasing a flood of excited children and tired parent volunteers.

The Youth Pastor, Ethan Parker, exited last, his boyish face contrasting with his 29 years. With tousled brown hair and boundless energy, he effortlessly connected with children of all ages. He gave James a mock salute before turning to help unload the luggage. "Troops delivered, Captain!" Ethan called. "Only three bathroom stops and one near-mutiny when the snacks ran out."

The retreat's grounds quickly changed from peaceful to lively chaos. Children raced around, exploring every corner, while parents coordinated cabin assignments and schedules. James moved through the crowd, greeting families and answering questions, the familiar weight of responsibility resting on his shoulders. By late afternoon, everyone had settled into their accommodations, and the group gathered in the dining hall for dinner. Long wooden tables quickly filled with chattering families, with the aroma of hearty stew and fresh bread warming the space.

James stood to deliver the welcome blessing as the room gradually quieted. "Let us pray," he began, and heads bowed. "Heavenly Father, we thank You for this sacred place, for the beauty that surrounds us, and for this time set apart. We ask that You open our hearts to hear Your voice in the whispers of these mountains, in the laughter of our children, and in the stillness of our spirits. Bless this food and our time together. In Your name, Amen."

A collective "Amen" rippled through the room, and dinner began with the clatter of utensils and the hum of conversation. James found himself observing the different family groups—the Andersons with their four lively children; the elderly Mrs. Patel with her daughter's family; the recently divorced Mr. Winters trying to connect with his withdrawn teenage daughter. Each person carried their own burdens and hopes to this mountain.

As the meal went on, James saw Michael moving among the tables, apparently making friends with everyone. The boy had a natural charm, engaging both adults and children with his curious questions and friendly smile.

Later, as twilight descended, the group moved to the outdoor amphitheater. Stone benches arranged in semicircles faced a central fire pit, with the mountains turning purple in the fading light as a backdrop. Thomas had prepared a magnificent fire that sent sparks dancing toward the emerging stars.

This was James' favorite part of each retreat—the first night's gathering, where the tone was set. Ethan led the children in lively songs, complete with hand motions that encouraged even the most reserved adults to join in. The mountains seemed to cradle their voices, amplifying them toward Heaven. When the singing ended, James stepped forward. The firelight cast flickering shadows across the gathered faces, all expectant and open. "Look around you," he began softly, causing people to lean forward to hear. "What do you see?"

"Trees!" called out a small voice that James recognized as Michael's.

"Mountains!" offered another child.

"Stars!" said another.

James nodded. "Yes, God's creation is all around us. But I'm talking about something even more miraculous. I'm talking about you. Each of you, created in God's image, carrying His spark within you." He paced slowly around the fire. "This weekend, we'll be exploring what it means to recognize the divine whispers in our lives—those moments when God speaks through circumstances, through Scripture, and through each other." He paused, looking at the children's upturned faces. "Sometimes, those whispers come in unexpected ways, through unexpected messengers." He then continued his message, weaving Scripture with personal stories, careful to keep his words accessible to the youngest listeners while still meaningful to the adults. As he spoke, he noticed Thomas standing at the edge of the gathering, arms crossed, his expression unreadable in the shadows.

After the service, families headed to their cabins. The children's energy finally faded as the day's excitement gave way to fatigue. James stayed by the fire, talking quietly with parents and addressing their concerns.

"That was a beautiful message, Pastor," Rebecca said as she approached with a sleepy Michael in tow. "I especially appreciated your words about finding God in the darkness. After David died, there were moments when I couldn't feel God's presence at all. But He was always there, working in ways I couldn't yet see."

"Mom, can I get some hot chocolate before bed?" Michael interrupted, stifling a yawn.

Rebecca checked her watch. "It's getting late, sweetheart. We should head to our cabin now."

"I'll walk with you," James offered. "I need to check on the boys' cabins anyway."

They strolled through the grounds, with Michael running ahead despite his earlier fatigue. The night had fully fallen now, with mist starting to curl around the base of trees. Path lights cast a gentle glow, illuminating the way while preserving the sacred darkness of the mountain night.

"This place has history," James said quietly to Rebecca. "Almost half a century as a spiritual retreat. Many lives have been changed on this mountain."

"I can feel it," she acknowledged. "There's something about being away from everyday distractions. It's easier to hear God."

They reached the fork in the path where they would separate—Rebecca and Michael heading toward the female guests' cabins, James toward the males'.

"Goodnight, Pastor James!" Michael called, suddenly remembering his manners.

"Goodnight, Michael. Remember, breakfast is at 7:30. The first one there gets the chocolate chip pancakes!"

The boy's eyes widened at the stakes. "I'll be there at seven!"

As Rebecca led her son down the path, James watched them go, a strange uneasiness washing over him. He shook it off, blaming it on the responsibility he felt for every soul under his care this weekend. He finished his rounds, checking each boys' cabin to ensure the younger ones were settling in and that the parent volunteers had everything they needed. When he finally returned to the main grounds, most lights had been turned off, leaving only security lighting and the distant glow from the main lodge where Thomas and Eleanor would be staying.

Near the dining hall, James noticed a figure standing motionless, staring into the darkness at the edge of the woods. As he got closer, he recognized Ethan's lanky frame. "Everything okay?" he asked softly.

Ethan was surprised by James' sudden appearance. "Oh, Pastor James. Yes, just... taking it all in." He gestured vaguely toward the forest. "I thought I saw someone out there, but it was probably just deer. They come right up to the buildings sometimes."

James peered into the darkness but saw nothing. "All the children accounted for?"

"Yes, sir. Tucked in, and most are already asleep. The bus ride wore them out."

"Good." James patted Ethan on the shoulder. "Get some rest. Tomorrow's busy schedule begins early."

Ethan nodded but seemed hesitant to move. "Pastor James," he said cautiously, "have you ever felt like... like you're exactly where you're supposed to be, but also like something doesn't feel right?"

The question caught James off guard. "That's an interesting way to put it. Are you feeling that way now?"

Ethan shook his head and let out an awkward laugh. "Ignore me. It's just the mountain air making me philosophical. Goodnight, Pastor."

As Ethan walked away, James once again turned toward the dark tree line. The night had grown deeper, and the mist thickened into tendrils that seemed to reach with spectral fingers across the ground. The mountains, which appeared so welcoming in daylight, now loomed like silent watchers. For a brief moment, James understood exactly what Ethan meant. Mount Hermon Retreat Center was, indeed, sacred ground—a thin place where Heaven felt closer. But as any theologian knew, where the divine nears, other forces often contest the space.

'Whispers of the Divine,' James thought, recalling his sermon title. *'But sometimes, other things whispered, too.'*

With that disturbing thought, he moved toward his cabin, unaware that in less than 24 hours, this serene mountain escape would become the heart of a nightmare, testing not only his faith but also the very core of his identity and purpose.

Chapter 2: The Vanishing

Morning arrived at Mount Hermon with a gentle persistence, the mist rising from the valley as sunlight crept over the eastern ridge. Pastor Miller had been awake since five, his old police habits still governing his internal clock after all these years. He sat on the small porch of his cabin, Bible opened on his lap, a steaming mug of coffee warming his hands against the mountain chill. This quiet communion before the day began was sacred to him—a time to center himself before shepherding others. But this morning, his prayers kept dissolving into fragmented thoughts, his mind returning to Ethan's strange comment from the night before and his own unsettling feeling when he'd looked out toward the darkened woods.

A distant door slammed, followed by the pitter-patter of eager footsteps on the path. James checked his watch. 6:45 a.m. Only one person would be up this early with such enthusiasm.

"Pastor James!" Michael called out as he skidded around the corner, still in pajamas with a hoodie hastily pulled over them, sneakers unlaced. "I'm first for pancakes, right?"

James couldn't help but smile. "The dining hall doesn't open for another 45 minutes, Michael."

The boy's face flickered with disappointment for a moment before it lit up again. "But I'm still first, right? Nobody else is even up!"

"You are definitely first," James confirmed, closing his Bible. "Where's your mom?"

"Getting dressed. She said I could come find you if I promised not to bother anyone else." Michael hopped from one foot to the other, unable to contain his energy. "Can I sit with you until breakfast?"

James patted the wooden step beside him. "Pull up a seat. But you might find it boring—just an old man and his coffee."

Michael sat, immediately noticing the Bible. "Were you talking to God?"

The straightforwardness of children never ceased to amaze James. "In a way. I was reading His words and thinking about what they mean for us today."

"Does God have a special voice when He talks to you? Mom says sometimes, He whispers so quietly, you have to really pay attention."

James thought about this. "Your mom is very wise, Michael. God speaks in many ways—through Scripture, through other people, through circumstances. The trick is learning to recognize His voice among all the other noise."

Michael nodded knowingly, as if this confirmed a personal theory. "That's why we came to the mountain, right? Less noise?"

"Exactly right, young man," James said, impressed by the child's insight.

They sat in comfortable silence for a moment, watching a pair of brightly colored cardinals dart between dark green pine branches.

"I had a dream about my dad last night," Michael said suddenly, his voice quieter. "He was trying to tell me something important, but I couldn't hear him."

James felt his chest tighten. He'd counseled enough grieving families to understand the significance of this moment. "Dreams can be one way we process our thoughts and feelings, especially about people we miss."

"Do you think God lets people in Heaven send us dreams?" Michael asked innocently.

The theological implications were complex, but James sensed the boy needed something simpler than doctrine right then. "I think God understands how much we miss the people we love. And while I don't know exactly how Heaven works, I believe God sometimes comforts us with reminders of those people."

Michael appeared to seriously consider that response before suddenly shifting the topic with the carefree spirit of childhood. "Did you know there are 27 different kinds of salamanders in these mountains? I read about them in my animal book."

Before James could respond, Rebecca appeared on the path, looking a bit frazzled. "Michael Chen! I told you to find Pastor James, not to run off without telling me where you were going." Her tone was stern but carried the anxious undertone of a parent who had already lost someone.

"But mom, I did find him! And I'm first for chocolate chip pancakes!"

Rebecca's expression softened as she approached. "I'm sorry, Pastor. He was gone before I finished brushing my teeth."

"No harm done," James assured her as he stood. "We were having a theological discussion about divine communication and amphibians," he said with a hearty laugh.

The dining hall quickly filled with retreat attendees. The air was rich with the scent of coffee, pancakes, and bacon. True to his promise, James made sure Michael got the first stack of chocolate chip pancakes, much to the boy's delight.

The morning unfolded as planned: breakfast, followed by a devotional period led by Ethan, then the group divided into age-appropriate activities. James moved between groups throughout the morning, watching Ethan lead the children in games designed to teach biblical concepts, while Thomas guided the adults in a more advanced study on hearing God's voice in a noisy world. The morning air was cool but pleasant, filled with laughter and conversations that blended with the natural symphony of birds and rustling leaves.

At noon, everyone gathered again for lunch, with the children excitedly sharing stories of their morning adventures. James saw Michael at a table with two other boys around his age, gesturing animatedly while talking, his sandwich momentarily forgotten.

"He's quite the social butterfly," Eleanor commented, following James' gaze as she set her tray beside him. "Asked me at least 15 questions during crafts time. That boy's mind never stops."

"Rebecca mentioned he's been seeing a counselor since his father's passing," James replied quietly. "He seems to be adjusting well."

Eleanor's eyes softened. "Children are remarkable that way. They process their grief differently than we do. It comes in bursts rather than the constant weight adults carry." She took a bite of her salad before adding, "Speaking of carrying things, have you noticed that Thomas seems... burdened this weekend?"

James had, indeed, noticed. Throughout the morning, the deacon had performed his duties flawlessly, but there was a distraction in his eyes and tension in his shoulders. "Family troubles, maybe. His daughter's divorce was finalized last month."

"Perhaps," Eleanor said, though her tone suggested skepticism. "Or perhaps it's the Peterson matter affecting him."

"The Peterson matter?" James asked, frowning.

Eleanor looked genuinely surprised. "The church board didn't tell you?" James shook his head no. "Well, Lawrence Peterson is threatening to sue the church over that youth center property donation. Claims his father wasn't of sound mind when he bequeathed it." She shook her head. "Thomas has been handling the legal aspects as our resident attorney."

This news came as a surprise to James, and the fact that it had been hidden from him was upsetting. Before he could ask more, Ethan came to their table with a clipboard. "Pastor, quick question about the afternoon schedule. The weather report predicts thunderstorms around four. Should we move the outdoor activities earlier?"

James checked his schedule. "Good thinking. Let's swap the hiking with the indoor prayer stations. Please notify the group leaders." As Ethan left, he noticed Michael exit the dining hall, followed by his two new friends. Through the window, he watched the boys head toward the recreation field where other children were already gathering for the afternoon activities.

The afternoon went smoothly despite the schedule change. Around 3:00 p.m., clouds started gathering over the western ridge, with their billowing tops illuminated by the sun while their bases darkened ominously. James helped Ethan corral the children from the field back toward the main lodge as the first distant rumble of thunder reached them.

The approaching storm set a perfect mood for the prayer stations arranged throughout the main building. Each station focused on a different aspect of prayer—thankfulness, intercession, confession, and listening—with age-appropriate activities provided at each. Families moved through the stations at their own pace, with dim lighting and soft background music creating a reflective environment that even the most energetic children seemed to respect.

James observed from the perimeter, occasionally offering guidance or answering questions. He saw Rebecca at the listening prayer station, eyes closed, with a peaceful expression on her face. He didn't see Michael right away but assumed he was with the other children at the more interactive stations.

By five o'clock, the storm had fully arrived. Rain pounded against the windows, and lightning lit up the darkening sky. The prayer session ended, seamlessly transitioning into dinner time. The dining hall filled with the comforting sounds of people sharing meals amid the storm's intense backdrop.

James noticed Rebecca entering the dining hall, looking around expectantly. When their eyes met, she approached his table. "Have you seen Michael? He was with the Sanderson boys earlier, but they said he went to find me about an hour ago."

"I haven't," James replied, a slight uneasiness stirring. "Let me check with Ethan. He was overseeing the children's prayer stations."

Ethan was helping serve at the buffet line. When asked about Michael, he shook his head. "The last time I saw him was at the thankfulness station, maybe 45 minutes ago? He made a beautiful card for his mom."

Rebecca's expression tightened almost imperceptibly. "I'll check our cabin. Maybe he went back for something."

"And I'll check the boys' side," James offered. "He might have gone with his friends."

They parted at the dining hall exit, with Rebecca rushing toward the girls' cabins while James headed for the boys' area. The rain had eased to a steady drizzle, but darkness was falling quickly, sped up by the storm clouds. James moved efficiently from cabin to cabin, checking in with parent volunteers. None had seen Michael since the prayer activity.

When James returned to the dining hall 15 minutes later, Rebecca was already there, her face now showing clear concern. "He's not in our cabin, and I've checked the bathrooms and craft area," she reported.

James maintained a calm exterior, although experience told him they should expand the search immediately. "Let's be systematic. Ethan," he called to the youth pastor, "can you check all the activity rooms in the main lodge? Eleanor, please stay here in case Michael shows up for dinner. Thomas, can you check the chapel and surrounding areas?"

The small search party dispersed efficiently. James turned to Rebecca, whose breathing had quickened. "We'll find him, Rebecca. Children wander off all the time at these events.

He probably found a quiet place to read or maybe fell asleep somewhere."

She nodded, clearly trying to believe him. "Should I check the lake? He was fascinated by it yesterday."

"The lake is off-limits without supervision, and the gates are locked," James assured her, even as a chill ran down his spine at the thought. "But let's check the path that overlooks it. He might have gone to watch the storm over the water." They hurried together through the drizzle, calling Michael's name. The path to the lake overlook was muddy, but it showed no signs of small footprints. Other parents had joined the search, spreading out across the grounds, their flashlight beams cutting through the gathering darkness.

Thirty minutes later, as the search party regrouped at the main lodge with no sign of Michael, James felt the first genuine sense of alarm. The retreat center covered nearly 40 acres, much of it wooded. A child could easily get disoriented, especially in fading light and unfamiliar surroundings.

"He wouldn't just wander off," Rebecca insisted, her calm façade cracking. "He knows better. Something has to be wrong."

James made a quick decision. "Thomas, call the local sheriff. Report a missing child." The words felt heavy as he spoke them, memories from his police days surfacing unbidden. "Everyone else, let's organize into search teams. Each team needs at least one flashlight and one cell phone."

The atmosphere shifted instantly. The casual worry of adults searching for a wandering child turned into something more urgent, more primal. Parents instinctively pulled their own children closer, counting heads and reassuring themselves that their families still remained intact.

Within minutes, Thomas returned from making the call. "The sheriff says they're sending deputies, but it might take 30 minutes or more on account of the mountain roads and weather."

"We can't wait that long," James said decisively. "Ethan, take a team and check the north trail. Thomas, you know the east side best. Eleanor, stay here to coordinate and maintain a point of contact. Rebecca will come with me to the south trail. Michael might respond better if he hears his mother's voice." As people moved with a new purpose, James pulled Thomas aside briefly. "Check the maintenance shed and staff quarters, too. Leave no building unopened."

Thomas nodded grimly. "You think this is more than a child wandering off, don't you?"

James hesitated, his police instincts warring with his pastoral restraint. "I think we cover all possibilities. Statistically, he's most likely sheltering somewhere from the rain. But we treat this seriously until we know otherwise."

With flashlights in hand, James and Rebecca headed into the woods along the south trail, calling Michael's name every few yards. The rain had stopped entirely now, but water still dripped continuously from the saturated tree canopy above. Their flashlight beams illuminated the shiny, wet surfaces of leaves and tree trunks, creating an eerily beautiful scene that sharply contrasted with their growing fear.

"Michael is smart," Rebecca said between calls, as much to reassure herself as to inform James. "If he got lost, he'd know to stay put and wait for help. We taught him that after... after his father died. Emergency preparedness became important to me."

19

James nodded and scanned the underbrush carefully. "That's good, Rebecca. Makes him easier to find." They kept going for another ten minutes before James' flashlight hit something bright on the dark forest floor. He moved closer, with Rebecca following anxiously.

It was a tiny plastic keychain—a miniature turtle.

Rebecca's sharp intake of breath confirmed its significance before she spoke. "That's Michael's. David gave it to him on his sixth birthday. He never goes anywhere without it."

James knelt to examine the muddy ground around the keychain. His police training, although dormant for years, reactivated with disturbing ease. The heavy rain had obscured most signs, but there was an impression in the mud that could have been a small footprint. Next to it was a larger, deeper impression. "Rebecca," he said carefully, "did Michael mention making any adult friends here? Someone who might have invited him to see something in the woods?"

Her eyes widened with new fear. "No. He's cautious with strangers—another thing we emphasized after losing David." Her voice broke slightly. "Pastor James, you don't think..."

He stood, pocketing the keychain. "I don't think anything is definitive yet. But we need to expand our search and get the sheriff here as quickly as possible."

As they turned to head back to the main grounds, a shout echoed through the trees. James recognized Ethan's voice, coming from somewhere to their right, off the trail. Without hesitation, he and Rebecca moved toward the sound, branches whipping at their faces as they left the path. They found Ethan standing in a small clearing about 50 yards from the trail, his flashlight trained on the ground. As they approached, James saw what had caused Ethan's shout: a child-sized shoe—Michael's distinctive red sneaker, abandoned in the mud.

Rebecca made a sound that seemed to come from somewhere deeper than her throat—a primal recognition of threat to her child.

"There's no blood," James said quickly, examining the area. "No signs of a struggle." But even as he spoke those reassuring words, his trained eye caught other details—broken branches at adult height, not child height; a clear path of disturbance leading deeper into the woods; a small, colorful thread snagged on a thorny bush that matched the sweater Michael had been wearing earlier. "Call Thomas," James instructed Ethan, his voice dropping into the authoritative tone he hadn't used since leaving the force. "Tell him to inform the sheriff that we now have evidence suggesting a possible abduction. Then, get everyone back to the main lodge for a headcount. I want to know every person who is on this mountain right now."

Ethan's face had gone pale, but he nodded and pulled out his phone.

Rebecca stood motionless, staring at her son's abandoned shoe. "Someone... took... him," she whispered. "Someone took Michael."

James placed a steady hand on her shoulder, even as his mind began cataloging suspects, scenarios, and timelines. "We don't know that for certain, but we're going to find him, Rebecca. I promise you that." The words echoed in the silent forest. They formed a pastor's promise that now carried the weight of his former oath to protect and serve.

As distant sirens started wailing on the mountain road, James realized that the peaceful spiritual retreat had become something entirely different—a crime scene where the whispers of the Divine had to compete with the darker forces of human nature.

And somewhere in the vast darkness of the surrounding forest, eight-year-old Michael Chen was missing, his absence tearing a hole in the fabric of safety that Mount Hermon Retreat Center had always represented.

The sanctuary has been violated.

The ground defiled.

And the nightmare was only beginning.

Chapter 3: Earthly Authorities

By midnight, Mount Hermon Retreat Center had completely transformed. The sacred sanctuary space now pulsed with the harsh blue and red lights of patrol vehicles. Yellow crime scene tape cordoned off the south trail, and uniformed deputies moved with methodical precision through areas where children's laughter had echoed just hours before.

In the main lodge, Rebecca sat motionless on a worn leather sofa, an untouched cup of tea growing cold between her hands. Pastor James stood nearby, watching through the window as another vehicle wound its way up the mountain road, this one unmarked.

"They've called in the county detective," Sheriff Larson explained, following James' gaze. The sheriff was a broad-shouldered man in his mid-50s with deep creases around his eyes that spoke of both laughter and sorrow witnessed over decades of service. "Standard procedure for a missing child case, especially with the evidence suggesting..." He glanced at Rebecca and diplomatically amended his words. "Given the circumstances."

James nodded, appreciating the sensitivity. In the three hours since they found Michael's shoe, the local authorities responded with commendable efficiency. The retreat grounds were secured, all attendees accounted for and briefly interviewed, and a preliminary search of the surrounding woods was conducted; however, darkness and wet terrain limited the effectiveness of the latter.

"Detective Collins is good," Sheriff Larson continued quietly. "Former FBI. Moved here two years ago for her own reasons. Keeps to herself mostly. Goes to that little church in Riverdale. But when it comes to cases involving children, there's nobody better."

The unmarked vehicle parked, and a woman emerged, her movements precise and economical. Even from a distance, James could see the focused intensity in her bearing as she conferred briefly with a deputy before striding toward the lodge. Detective Sarah Collins entered like a controlled storm—her presence immediately commanding attention without theatrical effort. She was in her early 30s, with dark hair pulled back in a practical ponytail, wearing a charcoal pantsuit that seemed explicitly chosen to deflect attention rather than attract it. Her eyes, a penetrating gray-blue, scanned the room, assessing and categorizing. "Ms. Chen?" Her voice was lower than expected, with a gentleness that contrasted with her otherwise businesslike demeanor. She crossed to Rebecca and knelt to be at eye level. "I'm Detective Sarah Collins. I'm going to find your son."

The simple statement, made without qualifiers or false comfort, seemed to resonate with Rebecca unlike any previous attempt. She looked directly at the detective—the first time she had looked anyone in the eyes since the shoe was discovered. "Someone took him," she said, her voice hollow but certain.

"We're investigating all possibilities, ma'am," Detective Collins replied, neither confirming nor denying the accusation. "I need to ask you some questions. Would you prefer to speak privately?"

Rebecca glanced at James. "Pastor Miller should stay. He was with me when we found... when we found the evidence."

Detective Collins' gaze shifted to James, her expression unreadable. "Pastor Miller. Sheriff Larson mentioned you have a law enforcement background?"

"Twelve years with Memphis PD," he confirmed. "Left the force seven years ago."

Something flickered briefly in her eyes—perhaps assessment or curiosity—before she shifted her focus back to Rebecca. She pulled out a small notebook. "Ms. Chen, tell me about Michael. Not just what he looks like or what he was wearing. Tell me who he is."

That seemed to breathe new life into Rebecca. "Michael is... curious. About everything. He asks questions most adults wouldn't think to ask. He's cautious with strangers but makes friends easily once he feels safe." Her voice grew stronger as she talked about her son. "He's sensitive—feels things deeply but tries to be brave. After his father died, he started keeping a notebook of 'evidence' that Heaven is real because he wanted me to have proof to comfort me."

Detective Collins wrote as Rebecca spoke, her expression professional but not detached. "What was Michael's state of mind today? Any unusual behavior, comments about meeting someone, secrets?"

"No. Nothing like that at all," Rebecca replied, shaking her head firmly. "He was excited about the retreat and making new friends. This morning, he was up before dawn to be the first in line for chocolate chip pancakes."

"And when did you last see him?"

"During the prayer stations activity around 4:15. He'd made me a card at one of the stations and wanted to show it to me, then he went back to finish another activity."

"Who else was with him at that time?"

Rebecca frowned, thinking. "Several children were moving between stations. The Sanderson boys—Jake and Tyler—said they were with him until he went to find me, but that would have been later, closer to five o'clock."

Detective Collins made a note. "Okay. I'll speak with them." She looked up. "Is there anyone who might want to hurt you through your son? Any custody issues, family conflicts, workplace problems?"

"No," Rebecca said firmly. "David's parents are in Seattle and were heartbroken about his death. They adore Michael. I work remotely as a graphic designer. No office conflicts. We've only been with this church for two years, but everyone has been nothing but supportive." Her voice cracked slightly. "Michael is all I have."

Detective Collins paused briefly before continuing. "I need to ask about the retreat itself. Was this a public event? Could someone have learned about it who wasn't a part of your congregation?"

At that, James stepped forward. "The retreat was announced in our bulletin and on our website, but registration was limited to church members and their invited guests. Everyone here should have a connection to someone in our church community."

"*Should have,*" Detective Collins repeated, emphasizing the uncertainty. "I'll need a complete list of attendees, including any last-minute additions or cancellations." She turned back to Rebecca. "Ms. Chen, we've arranged for a deputy to stay with you. I encourage you to try to rest, though I know that seems impossible right now. You'll help Michael most by keeping your strength up." After making sure Rebecca was settled with both the deputy and Eleanor for support, she gestured for James to follow her outside. The night air had grown colder, the earlier storm leaving behind a crystalline clarity that revealed stars in painful abundance. "You've maintained the scene where the shoe and keychain were found?" she asked without preamble.

"Yes. The deputies secured the areas immediately."

She nodded, professional but not entirely approving. "Walk me through the discovery. Every detail."

As they walked away from the lodge, James recounted the events that led to the discovery of Michael's belongings, being careful to distinguish between observation and interpretation. Detective Collins listened silently, her eyes constantly shifting, tracking details that most people would overlook.

"You said you were with Memphis PD," she said when he finished. "What division?"

"Started in patrol. Moved to Homicide after four years," James answered, the familiar ache of old memories stirring.

"You left to become a pastor." It wasn't a question, but her tone called for an explanation.

James hesitated. Most people received shortened versions of his story, but something about the detective's straightforward approach demanded complete honesty. "I worked a case—the Henderson kidnapping. A six-year-old boy taken from his bedroom. We found him three days later." He didn't go into detail about the condition in which they'd found the child. "I'd been questioning my faith for years, but that case broke something in me. Either God didn't exist, or, if He did, I couldn't understand a world He'd created where such things happened to children."

Detective Collins' steps slowed, but her eyes stayed fixed ahead. "Yet you became a pastor."

"Not immediately," he admitted. "I spent a year angry at God, at the world. Then I met a chaplain who didn't offer easy answers but helped me see that faith doesn't provide an escape from the world's darkness; it gives a light to carry into it."

She absorbed this without comment. After a moment, she asked, "Do you still think like a cop?"

"Tonight, I do," James acknowledged. "And since this is my retreat, my responsibility, and a child of my church member, I hope you'll allow me to help with your investigation in whatever way I can."

When they reached the edge of the woods where yellow tape marked the entrance to the south trail, Detective Collins stopped and turned to face James fully for the first time. "Pastor Miller," she began, her tone measured, "I appreciate your background and your personal investment in this case. But I need to be clear: this is my investigation. If you have any insights, I'd love to hear them. But I can't have a civilian—no matter how well-intentioned or experienced—conducting a parallel investigation or compromising evidence."

"I understand," he replied, meaning it. "My priority is finding Michael."

"As is mine," she affirmed. A brief silence stretched between them before she continued. "That said, you know these people. You know this place. I'd be foolish not to use you as a resource." It was as close to an olive branch as he suspected she ever extended. James nodded his acceptance of the terms. "I'd like to see where the shoe was found," she said, returning to business.

A deputy led them along the south trail to the small clearing where Ethan had found Michael's shoe. Crime scene technicians had set up powerful lights that turned the forest into an eerie scene.

Detective Collins moved methodically around the perimeter, her eyes tracking patterns invisible to the untrained observer. "What do you see?" she asked suddenly, not looking at James.

He blinked, surprised by the question. "You're asking for my assessment?"

"You have the training. And you were here first, before the scene was disturbed by well-meaning searchers."

James examined the area with renewed focus, setting aside his pastoral identity and channeling the detective he'd once been. "The broken branches are too high for a child moving alone. The pattern of disturbance suggests someone larger carrying something—or someone. The ground is wet from the storm, but there are no clear footprints leading away, which means either our suspect knew to be careful or they joined a more established trail where prints wouldn't be noticed."

Detective Collins nodded, neither confirming nor contradicting his observations. "And your impression of the timing?"

"Michael was last reliably seen around 4:15. The search started around 5:30. The window is narrow, especially since the storm was at its worst between 4:00 and 5:00." James frowned, a new thought coming to him. "The storm offered perfect cover—reduced visibility, people rushing between buildings, noise hiding any sounds."

"Almost as if someone knew the schedule and the weather forecast," Detective Collins murmured.

The implication hung in the air between them. James felt a chill that had nothing to do with the night air. "You think this was planned? Targeted?"

"I think," she replied carefully, "that random, opportunistic kidnappings rarely happen in remote locations during organized events with specific schedules." She turned toward the technicians. "I want casts of any partial prints you find, and thorough documentation of that thread and the disturbance pattern before this area is released."

As the pair walked back toward the main grounds, Detective Collins maintained thoughtful silence. James respected it, knowing the mental processes of assimilating initial evidence and forming preliminary theories. "I'll need to interview everyone," she said finally. "Starting with those who saw Michael last, then spreading outward. I've requested additional officers to assist. They'll arrive by morning. We'll also need search teams at first light, though I believe our best lead will come from the interviews."

James nodded. "I can help organize the search teams. Many of our church members are familiar with these woods from previous retreats."

They emerged from the forest to find the retreat center's grounds now fully illuminated by emergency vehicles and hastily erected floodlights. What had been designed as a place of spiritual retreat now resembled a military operation.

Near the dining hall, Ethan was talking with two deputies, his usual lively demeanor muted to something more serious. Thomas stood nearby, his posture stiff, arms crossed tightly over his chest. When he saw James and Detective

Collins, he moved quickly with purpose. "Pastor, the media has gotten wind of this situation," Thomas reported, his lawyer-like precision clear in his clipped tones. "There's a news van at the base of the mountain. The sheriff's deputies are stopping them from coming up, but they're asking for statements."

Detective Collins immediately stepped forward. "No statements except through official channels. Sheriff Larson will handle media coordination." She turned to James. "I understand your concern for your congregation, but controlling information flow is critical in the early stages of a missing child case."

"I agree," he said, surprising Thomas. "Our focus is supporting Rebecca and finding Michael, not managing public relations."

Thomas' expression tightened almost imperceptibly. "Of course. I merely thought you should be aware of all developments."

Detective Collins studied Thomas with that penetrating gaze of hers. "Mr. Webb, is it? I understand you're a church deacon and an attorney?"

"That's correct."

"I'd appreciate your help in setting up a temporary headquarters for our investigation. We'll need space for interviews, communications, and coordination."

The request—politely phrased rather than an order—appeared to redirect Thomas' energy toward a productive direction. "The conference room in the main lodge would work well. I'll handle it right away."

As Thomas walked away, Detective Collins shifted her focus to the dining hall, where Ethan was now accompanied by several other adults, all speaking in quiet, urgent tones. "That's the youth pastor?" she asked.

"Yes, Ethan Parker. He was coordinating the children's activities today and was part of the initial search party."

"I'd like to speak with him next," she said. Then, after a brief hesitation, she added, "You should get some rest, Pastor Miller. Tomorrow will be demanding."

James almost smiled at the suggestion. "With respect, detective, I won't be resting tonight. But I will stay out of your way unless you need me."

She looked him over quickly, then gave a slight nod of understanding. "One more question before I continue my interviews. In your professional opinion—both as a former law enforcement officer and as someone familiar with this community—is there anyone here I should especially consider speaking with?"

The question carried weight, and James thought about it carefully before replying. "Ethan Parker was one of the last to see Michael. He's devoted to the children, and they adore him, but he seemed on edge last night. Mentioned feeling that something wasn't right. Thomas Webb has been distracted this weekend. Apparently, there's a legal matter involving the church that I wasn't informed about." He paused. "And there's Martin Grayson, the retreat center's caretaker. He knows these grounds better than anyone and would have been aware of our schedule."

Detective Collins absorbed those details without revealing whether they aligned with her own assessments. "Thank you. I'll find you if I have additional questions."

As she walked toward the dining hall where Ethan waited, James was struck by the dichotomy she embodied—methodical and professional, yet with an undercurrent of intensity that hinted at personal investment beyond duty. He wondered about Sheriff Larson's comment that she attended "that little church in Riverdale" and how her faith influenced her work in the darker corners of human behavior.

The night seemed to stretch on endlessly. James moved between the command center set up in the conference room and the main lobby, where Rebecca kept her vigil, now surrounded by a small group of women from the church offering silent support. Around 2:00 a.m., he found himself standing at the edge of the parking area, surveying the retreat grounds now transformed by the investigation.

Eleanor appeared beside him, offering a steaming cup of coffee. "It's not your fault, James," she said quietly.

He accepted the coffee with a nod of thanks. "I'm responsible for this retreat, for these people."

"You're responsible for leading them. You're not responsible for the evil that others do." Her voice, typically brisk with practical efficiency, now carried the deeper wisdom of her decades of faith. "Even Jesus had a Judas among His disciples."

The biblical reference hung in the air between them, neither offering comfort nor condemnation, just acknowledging that even sacred spaces are not immune to darkness.

"What do you make of Detective Collins?" James asked, changing the subject slightly.

"Competent. Driven. And carrying something heavy." At James' questioning look, she elaborated. "I recognize the weight of private grief. I carried it myself after Harold died."

Before James could respond, a commotion arose near the main lodge. Detective Collins appeared, quickly heading toward a recently arrived vehicle. From it, a man in a suit carrying equipment cases stepped out, followed by two more officers in uniform.

"State investigators," Eleanor observed. "They're treating this as a priority."

James watched as Detective Collins conferred with the new arrivals, her posture conveying both respect for their authority and a protective stance regarding her case. After a brief discussion, she led them toward the conference room, glancing once in James' direction before disappearing inside.

Dawn was still hours away, but the investigation was already expanding with more resources being mobilized. In the growing law enforcement presence, James recognized both hope and warning: they were taking Michael's disappearance with the utmost seriousness, which meant they, too, believed this was not just a case of a child who had simply wandered off.

As if reading his thoughts, Eleanor spoke softly. "The Lord is close to the brokenhearted and saves those who are crushed in spirit."

"Psalm 34. I've quoted it to countless grieving families," he replied with a sigh.

"And believed it?"

"Yes," he said after a moment. "But believing God is present in suffering doesn't make the suffering easier to bear."

Eleanor's face showed no judgment, only understanding. "That's why He gave us each other. So that no one bears it alone."

From the main lodge, Rebecca emerged, wrapped in a borrowed blanket, her face pale but composed. She walked directly to where James and Eleanor stood. "They want me to record a statement," she said, her voice steadier than it had been earlier. "For the missing child alert that they will issue at dawn. I need... I need to be strong for Michael." Her eyes sought James'. "Will you pray with me first? Not the gentle, comforting prayer. I need the kind that storms Heaven's gates."

James felt something shift within him. He took Rebecca's cold hands in his. "Eleanor, will you join us?" The three formed a small circle at the edge of the chaos, heads bowed. When James spoke, his voice carried the dual authority of his callings:

"God of justice and mercy, we come before You now, not with gentle whispers but with the cries of those who seek Your divine intervention. Michael Chen is missing, taken by human hands, but not beyond Your sight. We ask not for comfort in our uncertainty but for Your power to be made manifest in bringing him home safely. Sharpen the minds of those who search, expose the plans of those who have taken him, and protect Michael with Your mighty hand. We declare that no weapon formed against him shall prosper, and we stand firm on Your promise that You are close to the brokenhearted. Give Rebecca supernatural strength and peace beyond understanding. In the powerful name of Jesus, Amen."

"Amen," Eleanor and Rebecca echoed, the latter's voice strengthened.

When they raised their heads, James noticed Detective Collins standing a short distance away, watching them with an unreadable expression. When their eyes met, she gave a slight nod—not of faith necessarily, but of respect for theirs—before turning back toward the investigation that would continue through the night and into what promised to be a long and grueling day ahead.

The earthly authorities had arrived in force, bringing resources, expertise, and determination. But as James looked at the stars still visible above the harsh artificial lights, he was reminded that higher authorities were also being petitioned—and it would take both Heaven and Earth working in concert to bring Michael Chen home safely.

Chapter 4: Faith Tested

Dawn broke over Mount Hermon with brutal beauty. The storm had washed the world clean, leaving behind a crystalline clarity that seemed to mock the chaos unfolding across the retreat's grounds. Sunlight spilled over the eastern ridge, illuminating dew-drenched grass and the faces of searchers gathering in the parking area, their breath forming clouds in the chilly morning air.

Rebecca stood at the edge of the assembled group, her petite frame nearly swallowed by a borrowed jacket too large for her shoulders. She hadn't slept. The deputies and church women who had stayed with her through the night could attest to that. She had alternated between pacing, praying, and silently staring out the window into the darkness that concealed her son.

Pastor James approached her, holding two steaming cups. "Coffee?" he asked, offering her one. "I remembered you like it black."

She accepted with a nod, her fingers curling gratefully around the warmth. "Thank you. Any news?"

"The search teams are organizing now. Detective Collins has a systematic grid mapped out, with priority areas based on..." He hesitated, not wanting to mention that the priorities were based on where bodies had been found in previous cases.

"Based on where a kidnapper might take a child," she finished for him, her voice hollow but unwavering. "You don't need to protect me from reality, Pastor. Reality took my son 18 hours ago."

James studied her face—the deep shadows beneath her eyes, the new lines etched around her mouth, the resolute set of her jaw. In those 18 hours, something fundamental had shifted in Rebecca. The quiet, faithful widow who found strength in gentle prayer had been replaced by a mother forged in fear's hottest fire.

"I should be out there," she said, watching as the first search teams received their assignments from sheriff's deputies. "Looking for him."

"Rebecca," James began carefully, "the best investigators in the county are working this case. The search teams are trained—"

"He's my son." Those three words contained multitudes—declaration, plea, accusation against the universe that had taken her husband and now threatened her child.

Before James could react, Detective Collins approached, her sharp appearance hiding the fact that she, too, had been working through the night. Only the faint redness in her eyes revealed her fatigue. "Ms. Chen," she greeted with a nod, then turned to James. "Pastor Miller. Thank you for organizing these volunteers. It's an impressive turnout."

Indeed, nearly every adult from the retreat had volunteered for the search, along with additional church members who had driven up at first light after hearing the news. They stood in a sea of determination—ordinary people preparing to do the extraordinary work of finding one small boy in miles of mountain wilderness.

"We've prioritized areas within a three-mile radius," Detective Collins continued, all business. "Each team has a deputy or officer assigned, along with someone familiar with the terrain. They've been briefed on what to look for and how to preserve any evidence they might find." Her gaze shifted back to Rebecca. "Ms. Chen, I've scheduled a press conference for 10:00 a.m. Your recorded statement will be released, along with Michael's photo and description. I'd like you to be present, but you don't have to speak if you don't feel up to it."

"I'll speak," Rebecca said immediately. "I want whoever has him to see my face. To know I won't stop looking."

Detective Collins nodded, a hint of approval flickering in her eyes. "We've also set up a tip line. Once Michael's information hits the media, we'll probably get dozens of calls. Each will be vetted."

As they spoke, a vehicle pulled into the parking area—an unmarked van with satellite equipment on the roof. A woman in a crisp black blazer emerged, followed by a cameraman and sound tech.

"Channel 5," Detective Collins identified. "The first of many. Sheriff Larson will coordinate with them, but I'd appreciate it if you could designate someone from your church to help with media relations, Pastor Miller. Someone with discretion and calmness."

"Eleanor," he replied without hesitation. "She'll keep them in line better than any deputy."

A faint smile touched the detective's lips. "I had the same impression." Her expression sobered as she turned back to Rebecca. "Ms. Chen, I need to speak with you about Michael's father."

Rebecca stiffened. "David died two years ago. Heart attack."

"I understand. But I need to verify that there are no custody complications or extended family members who might..." She left the implication hanging.

"Who might have taken my son," she replied flatly. "David's parents are in their 70s, living in Seattle. They video call Michael twice a month and send him books about animals. They're devastated about his disappearance and are flying in tomorrow. There's no one else."

Detective Collins nodded, making a brief note. "Thank you. I'll let you know immediately if the search teams find anything significant."

As she walked away, Rebecca's composure wavered for the first time, her hand trembling enough to slosh coffee over the rim of her cup. James gently steadied it.

"Rebecca," he said softly, "you don't have to be strong every minute. No one expects that."

"God does," she replied, her voice barely audible. "Job 13:15 — 'Though He slay me, yet will I trust in Him.'" Her eyes, when they met his, burned with desperate faith. "I've been reciting that all night because it feels like He's slaying me, Pastor. It feels like God has forgotten Michael. Forgotten me."

"He hasn't," James said, the clergyman in him responding automatically.

"Hasn't He?" The question carried no theatrics, only raw honesty. "First, David. Now, Michael. I've done everything right. I've believed. I've trusted. I've served. I've taught Michael to love Jesus above all else." Her voice cracked. "What more does God want from me? What more must I lose before He's satisfied?"

The theological answers James had been trained to give—about the fallen world, God's mysterious ways, and suffering's way of building character—all seemed hollow in the face of her anguish. Instead, he recognized what she truly needed at that moment. "I don't know," he admitted. "I don't know why this is happening. I don't know what God is doing. But I know He hears you. Your anger, your questions, your fear—He can bear it all."

Something shifted in Rebecca's stiff posture. Not relief, but the small surrender that comes with being truly seen during one's darkest moment. "I need to see the place," she said suddenly. "Where his shoe was found. I need to... I need to feel close to wherever he was last."

James hesitated, aware that Detective Collins would prefer the crime scene remain undisturbed except by investigators. However, he also understood a mother's primal need to connect with any trace of her child. "I'll take you," he decided. "But we'll need to stay on the perimeter. The evidence—"

"I understand," she interrupted. "I won't touch anything. I just need to see."

As they walked toward the south trail, James spotted Thomas engaged in a tense conversation with Ethan near the dining hall. The younger man's posture was defensive, with his hands gesturing emphatically, while Thomas remained impassive, arms crossed. Something about the interaction sparked James' old detective instincts, but before he could think about approaching them, Rebecca's voice drew his attention back.

"Did you mean what you said last night? In your prayer?" she asked. "About God's power being made manifest?"

James considered the question carefully. "I believe God can intervene supernaturally in human affairs, yes."

"But does He?" When it really matters?" The question cut to the heart of faith's greatest challenge. "Or does He just watch while people suffer?"

They finally reached the yellow crime scene tape that marked the entrance to the trail. James paused, searching for words that would be honest and hopeful. "In my experience," he said slowly, "God works both directly and through people. Through Detective Collins' training and intuition. Through search teams. Through you and me." He looked at her directly. "I've seen miracles, Rebecca. And I've seen tragedies where the miracle seemed absent. I don't have a formula for why some prayers are answered dramatically and others seem to go unanswered. But I do know this: God is as present in this moment as He was when He parted the Red Sea."

She absorbed his words, then ducked under the tape, moving carefully along the edge of the trail as James had indicated they should. They walked in silence until they reached the small clearing where Michael's shoe had been found. The crime scene technicians had finished their work hours earlier, but the area remained marked, with the disturbance pattern now outlined by small orange flags.

Rebecca stood motionless, her eyes taking in every detail. Then she closed them, her lips moving in silent prayer or perhaps simply communion with the last space her son had occupied. James remained respectfully silent, giving her this moment of connection. After several minutes, she opened her eyes. "He was scared," she said with quiet certainty. "I can feel the fear."

James didn't dismiss this as maternal imagination. In his police days, he'd learned to respect the inexplicable bond between parent and child. "What else do you feel?"

She frowned, concentrating. "Confusion. He wouldn't have gone willingly with a stranger. He knows better."

"Which suggests someone he knew," James said, thinking aloud. "Or someone who knew how to gain his trust quickly."

Rebecca's gaze sharpened. "Do you think it was someone from the retreat? From our church?"

"I think," he said carefully, "that Michael's disappearance shows planning and knowledge of the schedule. That narrows the possibilities."

Her expression hardened into something that dangerously resembled resolve. "Then we find out who." She turned, heading back toward the main grounds with renewed purpose. "I'm done waiting for 'updates.' I want to know everything the investigation has found."

James had to hurry to keep pace with her. "Rebecca, Detective Collins may not want to share details that could compromise—"

"I don't care what she wants," Rebecca interrupted, her voice tinged with an edge he'd never heard before. "My son has been missing for almost 24 hours. Every hour that passes..." She didn't finish the sentence. Didn't need to. They both knew the statistics on child abductions.

When they returned to the main grounds, they found increased activity around the conference room that had been converted to the investigation's headquarters. Additional law enforcement personnel had arrived, and a digital whiteboard had been set up, visible through the window. On it was a timeline of Michael's last known movements and a map of the retreat grounds with search zones marked.

Before James could suggest a more diplomatic approach, Rebecca strode directly to the door and entered without knocking. James followed, expecting resistance from the officers inside. Instead, he found Detective Collins looking unsurprised, almost as if she'd been expecting this development. "Ms. Chen," she acknowledged. "I was about to send for you. We've found something I'd like you to identify."

On the table, a small plastic evidence bag held a colorful piece of paper. Rebecca stepped forward, her breath catching as she recognized it. "It's the card," she whispered. "The one Michael made for me at the activity station."

Detective Collins nodded. "It was found about half a mile from where his shoe was discovered, along what looks like a game trail leading toward the eastern property boundary." She pointed to a spot on the digital map. "It suggests a direction of travel."

"Who else knows about this?" James asked, his police instincts fully engaged now.

"Just the search team that found it and the people in this room," she replied. "I'm controlling information flow tightly. If our suspect is monitoring our investigation, I want them to be uncertain about what we know."

Rebecca stared at the card, a handmade creation of construction paper and crayons. Even from where he stood, James could see a child's drawing of what appeared to be two figures—one large, one small—holding hands beneath a bright sun. "He drew us," Rebecca said, her voice threatening to break. "He and I."

Detective Collins paused briefly to let this sink in before proceeding. "Ms. Chen, I'd like your permission to bring in specialized resources. The FBI has a child abduction rapid deployment team that could be here by this afternoon."

"Why haven't they been called already?" Rebecca demanded.

"Protocol requires certain thresholds to be met. We're at that threshold now, with physical evidence suggesting a clear abduction rather than a lost child situation." She hesitated, then added, "It also means this case will receive national attention."

"Call them. Call anyone who can help find my son."

Detective Collins nodded to a deputy, who immediately stepped out to make the call. "We're also examining items from Michael's cabin—his suitcase, books, and belongings he brought to the retreat. Sometimes, children leave clues unwittingly."

"What can I do?" Rebecca asked, a new intensity in her voice. "I can't just wait around while everyone else searches."

"Actually, there is something. We're constructing a detailed picture of every person at this retreat—staff, attendees, everyone. You've been a part of the church for two years. You might notice inconsistencies or unusual behaviors that others might overlook."

James recognized it was a strategic move—giving Rebecca a productive outlet for her energy, while possibly gaining valuable insights. Rebecca appeared to acknowledge this as well, but she accepted the opportunity nonetheless.

"I want to see your suspect list," she said directly.

"We don't have official suspects yet," Detective Collins replied smoothly. "But we do have a list of everyone present this weekend, with notes on their interactions with Michael." She gestured to a junior officer, who brought forward a tablet. "Perhaps you could review these and add any observations." As Rebecca took the tablet and sat at the far end of the conference table, the detective pulled James aside. "Pastor Miller," she said quietly, "I'd appreciate your insights on the prayer service scheduled for this evening. I understand the importance of supporting your congregation through this crisis, but I'm concerned about the security implications."

"You're worried our kidnapper might attend," James stated, following her logic.

"It would be consistent with certain offender profiles," she confirmed. "The chance to observe the chaos they've created, gauge the investigation's progress, perhaps even insert themselves helpfully into the search."

James considered this. "Canceling would raise questions, possibly alert the suspect that we're on to them."

"Exactly. So, I suggest you proceed, but with officers present and observing. You would need to be aware of their presence but avoid drawing attention to them."

"I can do that," he agreed. "Though I must warn you: this community knows each other well. Strangers will be noticed."

"We'll use plainclothes officers familiar with church settings," she assured him. "I'd also appreciate it if you could pay particular attention to anyone showing inappropriate emotional responses—either excessive distress beyond their connection to Michael, or, conversely, unusual detachment."

James raised an eyebrow. "You sound like you've done this before."

Something flickered across her face—a shadow of old pain she quickly suppressed. "I have. In my FBI days. Child abduction cases were... my specialty."

Before he could inquire further, the door opened, and Ethan entered. His typically cheerful face was drawn with exhaustion and worry. "Pastor James," he said, then noticed Detective Collins and added more formally, "Detective. I wanted to let you know the children's parents are asking about a prayer service for Michael. They also want to know what they should tell their kids."

James looked at Detective Collins, who gave a subtle nod. "We'll hold a service at 7:00 p.m.," he decided. "Age-appropriate—something that acknowledges their fears but reassures them of God's presence."

"And the search teams?" Ethan asked. "Should we call them back in for it?"

"No," Detective Collins quickly interjected. "The search must continue until darkness makes it unsafe. We'll rotate teams for breaks, but we will not pause the effort."

Ethan nodded, then hesitated, shifting his weight from one foot to the other. "I keep thinking about yesterday, trying to recall every detail. Michael was at my station, making a gratitude list around 4:15. He seemed happy, normal. Then he said he wanted to show his mom something and left. That's the last time I saw him." His voice cracked slightly. "I should have watched more closely. Made sure he got to her."

"You couldn't have known," James said gently.

"But I'm responsible for the children during activities," Ethan insisted. "If I'd just paid closer attention—"

"Mr. Parker," Detective Collins interrupted, her tone professional but not unkind, "second-guessing doesn't help us find Michael. What does help is precise information. I'd like you to walk me through the prayer stations setup—exact locations, visibility between stations, who was assigned where."

Her redirection worked, giving Ethan a constructive focus. "Of course. I have the floor plan in my notebook. Should I get it?"

"Yes, please. Meet me back here in 15 minutes."

When Ethan left, James noticed Rebecca watching their interaction intently, her eyes narrowed in thought. "What is it?" he asked, moving to sit beside her.

"Something's not right," she whispered. "Ethan's station was gratitude lists, but Michael made this card at the creative prayer station. That was Eleanor's station, on the opposite side of the room."

James processed the discrepancy. "You're sure?"

"Absolutely. Michael told me he made it at 'Miss Eleanor's special card station.' Those were his exact words."

James caught Detective Collins' attention and signaled her to come over. Rebecca explained the inconsistency again, watching as the detective's expression subtly changed. "Good catch," she said, making a note. "It could be simple confusion on Mr. Parker's part, given the stress, but we'll clarify."

"Or he could be lying," Rebecca said bluntly. "Why would he lie about where he last saw my son?"

"Let's not jump to conclusions," James cautioned, although his own police instincts had flagged the discrepancy as possibly important. "Memory is notoriously unreliable under stress."

Just then, Detective Collins' phone buzzed. She checked it, her expression tightening. "Excuse me. I need to take this." She stepped away, speaking in sharp, low tones.

Left alone for a moment, Rebecca turned to James. "I saw Thomas confronting Ethan earlier. They looked like they were arguing."

"I saw them, too," he admitted. "I don't know what it was about."

"Find out," Rebecca ordered, her voice firm with determination. "If someone from our church took my son, I want to know why. And I want them to face God's judgment before they face man's... or mine."

The fierceness in her tone was startling, especially coming from the usually gentle woman. James recognized it as a mother's protective rage. He also saw how her faith was evolving under the stress of this ordeal, from passive acceptance to actively demanding divine justice.

Detective Collins returned, her professional mask firmly in place, but a new urgency was evident in her movements. "Ms. Chen, we've received a development. One of the search teams has found what appears to be a makeshift campsite about two miles east of where the card was found. There are indications that someone spent the night there with a child."

Rebecca stood so swiftly that her chair toppled backward. "Michael? Is he—"

"The site is abandoned," Detective Collins said quickly. "But recently. We've found a juice box of the type packed for children at this retreat, and impressions in the ground that could match a child of Michael's size. I'm heading there now with the forensic team."

"I'm coming with you," Rebecca stated. It wasn't a request but a declaration.

Surprisingly, the detective didn't object. "We'll take the UTV. It's rough terrain." She turned to James. "Pastor, I'll need you to keep coordinating here. The press conference will go on as scheduled. Eleanor is already working with Sheriff Larson on it."

James desperately wanted to join them but recognized his responsibilities to the broader community. "Please keep me updated. Rebecca, I'll be praying continuously."

"Pray with *action*," she replied, her eyes burning with a faith tested by fire but not consumed. "David wrote in Psalm 144:1 that God trained my hands for war, my fingers for battle. I never understood that verse until now."

As they left, James found himself alone in the command center, surrounded by the technology of modern investigation. On the whiteboard, Michael's timeline stared back at him, the gaps in their knowledge represented by question marks and dotted lines. His eyes landed on the small evidence bag holding Michael's handmade card—a child's drawing of mother and son under a bright sun. The contrast between the innocent artwork and the harsh reality of its discovery as evidence in a kidnapping case hit him with physical force.

He closed his eyes, feeling the weight of his dual roles— pastor and former detective—converge in this crisis moment. When he opened them again, he had made up his mind.

Detective Collins was pursuing the physical evidence, using all the resources of modern law enforcement. Still, there were other avenues he could explore, thanks to his unique position: the subtle dynamics of relationships, the hidden histories, and the spiritual currents that might have played a part in this terrible event. He would respect the official investigation, but he would also utilize every tool available—those he had gained on the police force and those he had developed as a pastor—to find Michael Chen. As he left the command center, heading to the dining hall where he knew Thomas and several church elders had gathered, he felt the weight of Rebecca's words echo through him: Pray with *action*.

Faith was being tested on Mount Hermon—Rebecca's, the congregation's, and his own. But faith without works is dead, and James Miller intended his faith to be very much alive in the search for one small boy whose disappearance had transformed a spiritual retreat into a battleground between good and evil... both human and divine.

Chapter 5: Hidden Pasts

Detective Collins expertly navigated the UTV over the rough terrain, each jarring bump reminding her of the urgency at hand. Next to her, Rebecca grasped the safety bar, her focus fixed despite the bumpy ride. "We're approaching the site," the detective called over the engine's roar. "Remember, this is an active crime scene. You'll need to stay where I direct." Rebecca nodded in acknowledgment, her jaw set with determination. As they crested a slight rise, the detective turned off the engine. Ahead lay a small clearing, now busy with forensic activity. Yellow evidence markers covered the ground, and technicians in white paper suits carefully documented everything in sight. "Wait here. Let me speak with the team leader first."

As the detective conferred with the senior forensic technician at the edge of the clearing, her mind automatically catalogued details. The site had been selected carefully. It was sheltered by overhanging branches, near a small stream, yet hidden from any established trails. Not the work of an opportunistic kidnapper, but of someone familiar with these woods. 'What do we have?" she asked the technician.

"An impression of two people sleeping—one adult-sized, one child-sized," he reported. "Remnants of packaged food, including a juice box matching the brand served at the retreat. Some disturbed ground, suggesting a hasty departure, probably this morning."

Detective Collins nodded, her eyes scanning the perimeter. "Any indication of restraints used? Signs of a struggle?"

"None visible. The child-sized impression appears undisturbed throughout the night, suggesting the child either slept naturally or was..." He hesitated.

"Sedated," she finished grimly. "Prioritize the juice box for testing. Any identifiable footprints?"

"A partial boot print heading east. Men's size 11 approximately. We're making a cast now."

"Good work. Keep me updated on anything else you find." She turned and walked back toward Rebecca, who now stood rigid with tension, her eyes fixed on the scene. "Ms. Chen, we've found evidence suggesting Michael spent the night here, likely with one adult male. There are no signs of injury or struggle."

Rebecca's eyes darted to each evidence marker, searching for something recognizable. "He's alive?"

"The evidence suggests he was alive and relatively well as of early this morning," Detective Collins confirmed, careful not to overstate or understate the implications. "The campsite appears to have been abandoned in haste, possibly when the search helicopters began operations at dawn."

"So, he must still be nearby," Rebecca concluded, a desperate hope entering her voice. "The person couldn't have gotten far with him."

The detective neither confirmed nor denied this, aware that false hope could be just as cruel as no hope at all. "We're expanding the search radius based on this new information. Every available officer and K-9 unit is being deployed to the area."

Rebecca took a tentative step toward the clearing, then stopped, recalling the instructions about not entering the crime scene. "What's that?" she asked, pointing to a small yellow marker near what appeared to be the child-sized impression in the ground.

Detective Collins hesitated, then decided Rebecca deserved honesty. "A small stuffed animal. Partially hidden under the leaves."

"A turtle?"

"Yes. How did you know?"

"It's Shelly," Rebecca whispered. "The toy turtle that Michael's father gave him. He sleeps with it every night. He must have hidden it... left it as a clue." Her composure finally cracked, a sob escaping before she ruthlessly suppressed it. "He's so smart, my boy. He's trying to help us find him."

Sarah's training cautioned against emotional involvement in cases, but Rebecca's resilience made maintaining professional distance challenging. "Your son sounds like a remarkable child," she said quietly.

"He is," Rebecca replied, strength returning to her voice. "And he needs us to be just as smart." She surveyed the scene again. "Where would they go from here? If they left this morning, they couldn't have gotten far on foot. Not with an eight-year-old."

Detective Collins was impressed by Rebecca's ability to think analytically despite her distress. "That's exactly what we're determining now. Based on the terrain and the direction of the partial footprint, they appear to be heading toward the eastern property boundary. There's an old access road about three miles from here."

"They'd need a vehicle nearby," Rebecca reasoned. "With all the police activity, someone would have noticed a stranger's car parked near the retreat center."

"Unless it wasn't a stranger's car," the detective said, observing Rebecca's reaction carefully.

Understanding dawned in Rebecca's eyes. "You think it's someone connected to the retreat, don't you? Someone whose vehicle wouldn't attract attention."

"Honestly, it's one possibility we're investigating. For now, I need to get you back to the main grounds. The press conference is in 30 minutes, and your presence will be critical."

As they returned to the UTV, Detective Collins observed how Rebecca cast one final, lingering glance at the campsite. That look held all the anguish of a mother torn from her child—a pain she understood more deeply than Rebecca could know.

****

Pastor Miller found Thomas alone in the dining hall, reviewing documents spread out on a table. The deacon looked up as he approached, hurriedly gathering the papers into a folder. "James," he greeted, his voice carefully neutral. "Any updates on the search?"

"They found a campsite," he replied, watching Thomas' reaction closely. "Evidence suggests Michael was there last night."

Thomas' expression revealed genuine surprise, then relief. "Thank God. So, he's alive?"

"It appears so," James confirmed, taking a seat opposite Thomas. "But the site was abandoned this morning. They're still searching."

Thomas nodded, unconsciously straightening the folder in front of him. "The whole church is praying. We've established a prayer chain—someone praying every minute of the day and night until he's found."

"I appreciate that," James replied before deliberately shifting gears. "Thomas, I saw you speaking with Ethan earlier. It looked... intense."

The deacon's posture stiffened. "Just retreat business. Ensuring the remaining children are properly supervised during this crisis."

"It had nothing to do with the Peterson legal matter that Eleanor mentioned?"

Thomas' eyes flashed with momentary annoyance. "Hmph. Eleanor should be more discreet. But no, that's a separate church matter that has nothing to do with current events."

"As the Senior Pastor, I'd prefer to be informed about legal threats to our church," James pressed, his voice calm but insistent.

Thomas sighed, relenting. "Lawrence Peterson is contesting his father's bequest of the youth center property. Claims undue influence. It's baseless. The elder Peterson was of sound mind and had expressed his intentions for years. The board didn't inform you because we didn't want to burden you with something we can handle internally." He met James' gaze directly. "I assure you, it has absolutely no connection to Michael's disappearance."

"And what about your heated conversation with Ethan?"

A flicker of something—discomfort? rage? concern?—crossed Thomas' face. "Ethan has been... struggling recently.

Personal issues affecting his work. I was checking that he's stable enough to continue his duties during this crisis."

"What kind of personal issues?" James pressed, his pastoral concern now aligned with investigative interest.

Thomas hesitated, clearly weighing confidentiality against the circumstances. "Financial, mostly. He has mentioned debt problems and pressure from creditors. And there's a woman—someone from his past who's resurfaced recently."

This was news to James. Ethan had always seemed transparently open about his life. "He hasn't mentioned any of this to me."

"He's proud. Doesn't want to disappoint you. Look, James, I know your background makes you see suspects everywhere, but Ethan adores those children. He wouldn't harm a hair on Michael's head."

"I'm not accusing anyone," James clarified. "But in a situation like this, we need complete transparency. No hidden agendas, no secrets."

Thomas nodded slowly, then, after a moment's hesitation, asked, "Have you spoken with Martin Grayson yet? The caretaker of the property?"

"Not since yesterday morning. Why?"

"He was acting strangely last night. Eleanor mentioned seeing him load something into his truck around the time the storm began. When she asked what he was doing, he was evasive."

James felt a cold weight settle in his stomach. "His truck? Is it still on the property?"

"I haven't seen it today. But with all the emergency vehicles, I might have missed it," Thomas admitted.

James stood. "I need to tell Detective Collins. Martin knows every inch of these grounds. If he's involved..."

"Don't jump to conclusions," Thomas cautioned, echoing James' own earlier words. "But yes, the detective should know." As James turned to leave, Thomas called after him, "James? Whoever has Michael—they're not just committing a crime; they're committing a sin against God Himself. The Word says, 'Whoever causes one of these little ones to stumble, it would be better for him if a millstone were hung around his neck and he were thrown into the sea.'"

The biblical quote from Matthew 18:6 hung in the air as James nodded grimly and left to find Detective Collins.

****

The press conference took place on the steps of the main lodge—a surreal scene of tragedy displayed publicly. Sheriff Larson spoke first, clearly presenting the facts of the case. Detective Collins then followed, her commanding presence capturing the attention of the gathered reporters.

"Michael Chen is eight years old, approximately four feet tall, with black hair and brown eyes," she stated, standing next to an enlarged photo of the boy. "He was last seen wearing blue jeans, a green sweater with a dinosaur design, and red sneakers. One of those sneakers has been recovered during our search." The cameras flashed continuously as she spoke, recording every word and expression. "We are treating this as a child abduction case. The FBI Child Abduction Rapid Deployment Team has been activated and will arrive within hours. We have physical evidence suggesting Michael was alive as of this morning, and

58

we are pursuing multiple leads." She turned slightly. "Ms. Chen, Michael's mother, would like to make a brief statement."

Rebecca stepped forward, her small frame somehow amplified by the intensity of her purpose. She refused preparation or coaching, insisting on speaking from her heart. Now, facing the cameras that would broadcast her message nationwide, she drew a steady breath. "My son, Michael, is a bright, loving boy who asks questions about everything from salamanders to angels. He loves books about animals and making people laugh. He is the center of my world." Her voice stayed remarkably steady, her eyes locking directly on the camera. "To the person who has taken him: I don't know who you are or why you've done this, but I want you to know that Michael needs special medication for his allergies." This was a fabrication—a tactic Detective Collins had suggested to possibly improve the child's treatment. "He needs to take it daily, or he could have a severe reaction." She paused, then continued with quiet intensity. "I am praying for you. Not just for Michael's safe return, but for your soul. Because I believe even the darkest heart can be redeemed. Please, let my son come home to me."

As the press conference ended and the reporters headed off to file their stories, James approached Detective Collins, who was quietly talking with an FBI agent who had just arrived ahead of the main team. "Detective," he interrupted apologetically. "I have information about Martin Grayson, the retreat center caretaker."

She excused herself from the FBI agent and gave James her full attention. "What about him?" James relayed what Thomas told him about Martin's strange behavior and the missing truck. Her expression stayed neutral, but he could tell she was mentally adding this to her evolving case file. "We've been looking for Martin for routine questioning since this morning," she revealed. "His cabin is empty. Where's Thomas now? I need a full statement."

"In the dining hall. Detective, Martin knows these mountains well. If he's involved—"

"We don't jump to conclusions," she interrupted firmly. "But we pursue every lead. I'll speak with Thomas, then check if Martin's vehicle has been flagged in the system."

As she walked away, James saw Rebecca standing alone at the edge of the dispersing crowd, her public strength now waning as the cameras were gone. He approached her. "You were incredible," he said softly.

"I said what needed to be said," she replied, exhaustion evident in her voice. "James, I need to ask you something. The detective mentioned that the FBI agents arriving have special expertise. What exactly does that mean?"

James hesitated, unsure how much to reveal about the specialized nature of the FBI's Child Abduction Rapid Deployment Teams—their focus not just on recovery but also on the psychological profiling of offenders who target children. "It means they bring additional resources and specialized training," he said carefully.

Rebecca studied his face. "You're not telling me everything. Please, don't hide the truth from me. I need to understand what we're up against."

James sighed, recognizing her right to complete information. "The FBI team specializes in child abduction cases. They have protocols, databases of similar cases, and behavioral analysts who can help build a profile of the person who took Michael."

"Based on what they've found at the campsite, what type of person are they looking for?"

Before James could respond, Detective Collins came back, her face composed but her movements hurried. "Pastor Miller, Ms. Chen—we've spotted Martin Grayson's truck on highway camera footage heading east about two hours ago. There seems to be a child in the passenger seat."

Rebecca gasped. "Michael?"

"We can't confirm identity from the footage, but the size of the individual matches that of a child. I've issued an APB for the vehicle. Every law enforcement agency in three states is now searching for it."

"Who is this man?" Rebecca demanded. "Why would he take my son?"

Detective Collins exchanged a glance with James before responding. "Martin Grayson has been the caretaker here for eight years. No criminal record. However, we've just learned he was previously employed at a youth camp in Oregon that closed following allegations of misconduct. We're still gathering details."

The implication hung heavy in the air, unspoken but understood. Rebecca swayed slightly, and James quickly moved to steady her. "I want to see the footage," she insisted, her voice tightening again.

"Ms. Chen—" Detective Collins began.

"It's my son," Rebecca interrupted. "I'll know if it's him, even from a grainy highway camera. Believe me, I'll know."

After a moment's hesitation, Detective Collins nodded. "Come with me."

****

The command center had undergone a transformation with the arrival of FBI personnel. New equipment and expertise flooded in. A large monitor displayed the highway camera footage in question—a distant, slightly blurred image of a dark blue pickup truck. The timestamp showed 9:17 a.m.

Rebecca stared intently at the freeze-frame, at the small figure visible in the passenger seat. "Can you zoom in? Enhance it?" A tech nodded, manipulating the image. The quality degraded with magnification, but the figure became more distinct: a child-sized person with dark hair. "The sweater. It looks green. Michael was wearing green." She leaned closer. "I think... I think it's him."

Detective Collins nodded to the tech, who noted Rebecca's identification. "We've set up roadblocks on all major routes, and officers are checking secondary roads. Every available unit is involved in the search."

"I don't understand. Why would this man take my son? Did he... did he hurt other children at that other camp?"

"We don't have confirmed details yet," Detective Collins replied carefully. "The camp closed abruptly, and records are sealed because minors were involved. The FBI is working to access them now."

"But that's the assumption," Rebecca pressed. "That's why everyone is looking so grim. You think he took my son for..." She couldn't finish the sentence.

James stepped forward. "Rebecca, we don't know Martin's motives. We're exploring all possibilities."

"Pastor Miller is correct," the detective agreed. "In my experience, assumptions can blind us to evidence that doesn't fit our theory. We focus on finding Michael, not speculating about motives."

"What can I do? There must be something I can do for my son."

"Actually, there is," Detective Collins said. "The FBI behavioral analysts would like to speak with you. The more they understand about Michael—his personality, habits, how he might respond in various situations—the better they can predict possible scenarios and outcomes."

As Rebecca was led away to speak with the FBI team, Detective Collins turned to James. "Pastor, I need a moment of your time." She guided him to a quieter corner of the room, her expression grave. "There's something you should know, given your background and involvement in this case. We've received information that Martin Grayson legally changed his name 12 years ago. His previous identity is still being confirmed, but preliminary matches suggest he may have been investigated—though never charged—in connection with a child disappearance in Washington state."

James felt a cold dread settle in his stomach. "And you believe Michael is with this man, whoever he claims to be today."

"Yes, the evidence points in that direction. But there's something that doesn't add up. The behavior pattern is inconsistent. Child predators typically don't camp overnight with victims in the open. They seek secure locations immediately. And the truck—driving on main highways where cameras could catch him? It's incredibly reckless or..."

"Or what?"

"Or it's meant to be seen. To direct our attention away from something else."

The implication hung between them—the possibility that Martin Grayson was a convenient scapegoat, not the actual kidnapper.

Before James could respond, his phone vibrated with a text. He checked it, then looked at Detective Collins with renewed urgency. "It's from Eleanor. Ethan is missing. He was supposed to lead the children's prayer group 30 minutes ago, but he never showed up. No one can find him."

****

In a dark room miles away, Michael sat on the edge of a narrow bed, his small face lit only by the blue glow of a crescent moon-shaped nightlight. His eyes were red-rimmed from crying, but the tears had long since stopped, replaced by a cautious stillness that was beyond his years.

The room was simply furnished—a bed, a small desk, and a bookshelf with children's titles. There were no windows, just a single door that remained locked from the outside. It wasn't a horrible place, but it also wasn't home.

And he wasn't allowed to leave.

"I know my mom's looking for me," he whispered to himself, a mantra he'd been repeating since being taken. "She won't stop until she finds me." He reached under the pillow, touching the small cross necklace his mother had given him last Christmas. They hadn't found it when they'd taken away his shoes and checked his pockets.

In the silence, he could hear muffled voices arguing beyond the door—two adults, their words indistinct but their tones clear. One angry, one pleading. Then footsteps approached, and Michael quickly pretended to be asleep as the door creaked open.

"I know you're awake," a familiar voice said. "It's okay. I brought you some dinner."

Michael opened his eyes, squinting against the light from the hallway. "When can I go home? You said it would just be for one night."

"Soon," came the reply, unconvincing even to an eight-year-old's ears. "Things are... complicated. But you're safe here, I promise."

"My mom is scared. She needs me."

A long pause followed, heavy with what seemed like regret. "I know. And I'm sorry, Michael. I truly am. But this is bigger than just you and your mom. Sometimes... sometimes people must make difficult choices for the greater good."

"Pastor James says the greater good never comes from doing bad things," Michael replied, his child's wisdom cutting through adult rationalizations.

Another long silence followed. Then, softly: "Eat your dinner, Michael. And say your prayers tonight. God is watching over you, even here."

The door closed, the lock clicked, and Michael was alone again in the blue-lit darkness. He reached once more for his hidden cross, holding it tightly in his small hand.

"Mom's looking for me," he whispered again. "And God can see in the dark. He knows exactly where I am."

With that small comfort, he closed his eyes, not to sleep but to pray—with all the faith his eight years had accumulated—

that tomorrow would bring rescue, and that the person who had brought him to this strange place would have a change of heart.

He left the food on the tray untouched and went to sleep.

Chapter 6: False Witness

Night had fallen over Mount Hermon, turning the searchlights piercing the darkness into beams of desperate hope. What started as a coordinated investigation now stretched across several fronts: the ongoing mountain search, the statewide alert for Martin Grayson's truck, and the mysterious absence of Youth Pastor Ethan Parker.

Pastor James stood at the edge of the parking area, watching FBI agents methodically process Ethan's small hatchback, still parked where he had left it yesterday morning. The young pastor's cabin had yielded few clues. His phone was missing, but his wallet and credential badge remained on the nightstand. A half-empty coffee mug suggested a hasty departure.

"Thinking like a cop again?" Detective Collins' voice came from behind him.

James turned to see her approaching, her face tired but her eyes still sharp. "Hard not to," he admitted. "Two disappearances from the same retreat within 24 hours. The statistical probability of coincidence is—"

"Approximately zero," she finished. "We're considering multiple theories. Ethan might be involved in Michael's abduction, could be a second victim, or may have fled out of fear or guilt."

"Or some combination of those theories. What's the latest on Martin?"

"Highway patrol spotted a truck matching the description about 80 miles east. They're closing in, but we haven't confirmed it's him yet."

"Have you checked Ethan's phone records? Credit cards?"

"The FBI's handling it, Pastor. There's been no activity since yesterday afternoon." She studied him for a moment. "You knew him well?"

"I thought I did," James replied, the admission painful. "He joined our staff three years ago. Young, enthusiastic, the children adored him. Perfect references, seminary degree with honors." He shook his head. "But according to Thomas, he's been having financial troubles, and there's some woman from his past who's recently resurfaced."

"We're looking into both those angles," she assured him. "People keep secrets, Pastor Miller. Even from those they respect."

There was something in her tone that drew his attention. Was it perhaps a personal awareness of secrets kept and their consequences?

Before he could inquire further, Sheriff Larson approached, his expression grave. "We've got a situation. The state police have intercepted Martin's truck."

"And Michael?" Rebecca's voice came from behind them, startling all three. She had appeared silently, wrapped in the same borrowed oversized jacket, her face pale but composed.

Sheriff Larson hesitated, his discomfort evident. "Ma'am, perhaps you should—"

"Just tell me!"

The sheriff looked at Detective Collins, who gave a slight nod. "The truck was abandoned at a rest stop," he reported. "No sign of Martin or the child. But..." he hesitated again.

"But what?" Rebecca pressed.

"There was blood in the passenger seat. Not much, but enough to warrant testing."

She leaned on James for support, gripping his arm with unexpected strength. "Is... it... Michael's?" she asked, each word clear and deliberate.

"We won't know until the lab results come back," Detective Collins answered honestly. "A forensic team is processing the vehicle now, and we've expanded the search to the area around the rest stop."

Rebecca closed her eyes briefly, visibly steadying herself. "What else aren't you telling me? I can feel you're holding something back."

Detective Collins exchanged a glance with Sheriff Larson before replying. "A child's backpack was found in the truck. The description matches the one Michael brought to the retreat."

"I want to see it," Rebecca said immediately.

"Ms. Chen," Sheriff Larson began gently, "the backpack is evidence that needs to be processed—"

"I can identify if it's Michael's," she insisted. "And if there's anything unusual or out of place inside it. No one knows my son's belongings better than I do."

"She's right," Detective Collins agreed. "We can have her examine it under supervised conditions once it's been photographed and documented."

"Thank you," Rebecca said, the simple acknowledgment carrying the weight of a mother clinging to any connection, however tenuous, to her missing child.

"There's something else you should know. We've received information about Martin Grayson that complicates our initial assessment," Detective Collins said with a sigh.

James felt Rebecca tense beside him. "What information?" he asked.

"The FBI has accessed the sealed records from the Oregon camp where Martin previously worked," Detective Collins explained. "The allegations that led to its closure didn't involve him directly. In fact, he was the whistleblower who reported suspected abuse by another staff member."

James was surprised. "So, you mean to tell us he wasn't under suspicion there?"

"On the contrary, he was considered a key witness for the prosecution. The case was ultimately settled out of court, with the records sealed to protect the minors involved."

"But his name change," Rebecca said, confusion evident in her voice. "His disappearance with Michael..."

"The name change occurred two years before the Oregon incident. And while we still need to question him about Michael, the profile is shifting away from our initial concerns."

"What about the previous investigation in Washington state?" James asked, recalling their earlier conversation.

Detective Collins' expression tightened almost imperceptibly. "That's where things get complicated. We've confirmed Martin was questioned in connection with a child disappearance 15 years ago, but as a potential witness, not a suspect. The child was his neighbor's son. The boy was never found."

The implications of this new information were crucial. If Martin Grayson wasn't the predator they initially feared, his flight with Michael indicated something different—possibly protection instead of abduction.

"So, we're back to square one," Rebecca said despondently, voicing the frustration they all felt.

"Not exactly," the detective countered. "Every piece of information narrows the field, even when it eliminates a suspect. And now we have Ethan's disappearance to factor in, which might be connected."

A sudden commotion near the main lodge caught their attention. Eleanor was rushing toward them, her usual composed demeanor replaced by clear agitation. "James! James!" she shouted, slightly breathless as she reached them. "You need to see this. They're running a story on the news about Michael, but it's all wrong."

****

The television in the main lodge was surrounded by a small crowd of FBI agents, deputies, and retreat attendees. On the screen, a somber news anchor spoke beside a photo of Michael—his school portrait from the previous year.

"...sources close to the investigation suggest that the disappearance of eight-year-old Michael Chen may be connected to allegations of financial impropriety at First Community Church. The boy's mother, Rebecca Chen, has reportedly been assisting church leadership with accounting reviews in recent months..."

"What?!" Rebecca stared at the screen in shock. "That's a bald-faced lie! I've never touched the church's finances!"

The anchor continued: *"Anonymous sources claim that discrepancies in church funds were discovered shortly before the retreat, and that certain church officials may have had motives to silence potential whistleblowers..."*

"This is outrageous," Thomas sputtered as he joined the gathering. "Pure fabrication and potentially libelous. As church counsel, I'll be contacting their legal department immediately."

Detective Collins was already on her phone, stepping away to speak urgently with someone at the station. James watched the report continue with a growing sense of dread, realizing how quickly false information could derail their investigation and potentially endanger Michael. "Turn it off," he demanded when the anchor began speculating about "persons of interest" among the church leadership.

Eleanor complied, but the damage was already done. The retreat attendees were looking at each other with suspicion as whispers began to circulate.

"Everyone, please," James raised his voice to address the room. "That report contains numerous falsehoods. There are no 'financial improprieties' at our church, and Rebecca has never been involved in our accounting processes. This is irresponsible journalism at its worst."

"Then where did they get the story?" someone called from the back of the room.

"That's what we intend to find out," Detective Collins said, rejoining the group. "Sheriff Larson is contacting the station now. Meanwhile, I ask that everyone refrain from speaking to the media. Misinformation can severely hamper our efforts to find Michael."

The crowd slowly dispersed, but James realized the damage had already been done. Small groups of people kept whispering and glancing at Thomas, James, and especially at Rebecca, who stood stiff with shock and anger.

"I need to make a statement," Rebecca said suddenly. "To correct the record immediately."

"Ms. Chen," Detective Collins began cautiously, "while I understand your desire to address these falsehoods, engaging with the media directly might—"

"They're suggesting I was somehow involved in my son's kidnapping," Rebecca snapped. "That can't stand. Not for a minute longer."

James gently placed a hand on her shoulder. "Rebecca, Detective Collins is right. Engaging now might make things worse. Let's focus on the investigation, not the ugly rumors."

"The same investigation that now has the whole community suspecting church corruption?" she challenged. "How does that help find Michael?"

Before either James or Detective Collins could respond, Thomas stepped forward. "I have contacts at several reputable news outlets," he offered. "We can issue a formal statement refuting these claims without directly engaging with the station that aired them."

Detective Collins thought about this. "A single, coordinated statement could be effective. But it needs to be carefully crafted not to reveal details that could compromise the investigation."

"I'll help draft it," Thomas volunteered, his attorney's precision potentially valuable in such a delicate task.

As they began discussing the details of the statement, James noticed Eleanor standing slightly apart, her expression troubled beyond simple concern about the false news report. "Eleanor?" he asked softly, moving to her side. "What is it?"

She hesitated, glancing around to ensure no one was listening. "James, there's something you should know. About the church finances."

Dread nearly swallowed James whole. "What about them?"

"Nothing missing or improper," she quickly clarified. "But there have been... questions. From the auditing committee. About the youth center project."

"What kind of questions?"

"Discrepancies in the contractor billing. Thomas has been handling it—said it was just paperwork errors." She lowered her voice further. "But Ethan was on the committee. He's been asking to see the original documentation for weeks."

"And you're saying Thomas refused?"

"Not refused, exactly. Rather, delayed. Said the papers were at his home office." She looked very uncomfortable. "James, I would have told you sooner, but Thomas insisted it was a minor issue that didn't warrant troubling you."

Before he could respond, his phone buzzed with an incoming text. "It's from Ethan," he said, showing Eleanor the screen. A single message:

'Not what you think. Need to talk. No police. Riverbrook Bridge. Midnight. Come alone.'

Eleanor's eyes widened, almost bulging out of their sockets. "Are you going to tell Detective Collins?"

"I don't know," he admitted. "If Ethan knows something about Michael but is afraid to come forward officially..."

"It could be a trap," Eleanor warned. "Or he might be involved in the kidnapping."

"Or he could be trying to help," he countered, though uncertainty colored his voice. "I need to think about this."

Their conversation was interrupted when Detective Collins called James' name. He quickly put his phone away and joined the others, where Thomas was already working on a statement on his laptop. "Pastor Miller, we've just confirmed that the truck found at the rest stop is definitely Martin's. The crime scene units are processing it now."

"And the blood?" Rebecca asked, maintaining remarkable composure given the circumstances.

"Still waiting on lab results, but the preliminary report suggests it's not a large amount. Could be from a minor injury," Detective Collins reported.

"What about Michael's backpack?" James asked.

"Being transported here now. Ms. Chen, if you're up to it, we'd like you to examine it as soon as it arrives."

Rebecca nodded firmly. "I'm ready for whenever it gets here."

As the group continued discussing the response to the news report, James found his thoughts drifting back to Ethan's text. The young pastor's disappearance initially seemed suspicious, but with this new information about financial issues at the church, another possibility arose—perhaps Ethan had fled not out of guilt but out of fear. He excused himself, needing some space to think. He stepped outside onto the lodge's porch, where the night air carried the scent of pine and the distant sounds of ongoing search efforts. The moon had risen, casting a silver light across the mountains that had once seemed so peaceful and perfect for a spiritual retreat.

"Troubled thoughts, Pastor Miller?"

He turned to find Detective Collins joining him, her observant eyes missing nothing. "Just trying to make sense of everything," he replied cautiously.

She nodded and leaned against the porch railing. "In my experience, cases like this rarely make complete sense until they're resolved. Even then, sometimes the 'why' remains elusive."

"Is that what happened with your FBI cases?" he asked, testing the waters of her past.

A shadow crossed her face, quickly controlled. "Some of them. The ones that stay with you."

"Like the ones that made you leave the Bureau and move to a small-town church?" He hadn't intended to be so blunt, but his detective instincts were on full display now.

She turned to look at him directly, assessing him with that penetrating gaze. "You've been asking about me, I see."

"Actually, no. Sheriff Lawson mentioned you attended 'that little church in Riverdale' and that you had your reasons for leaving the FBI."

For a long moment, she said nothing, and James thought she might refuse the implicit question. When she finally spoke, her voice was quiet but steady. "Four years ago, I led the investigation into a child abduction in Maryland. An eight-year-old girl, taken from a church function. We did everything by the book. Built the profile. Followed every lead. I was convinced we were closing in."

James waited, sensing the weight of what was coming.

"We found her three days later. It was too late." Her professional façade cracked slightly, revealing a glimpse of old pain. "The worst part? I interviewed the perpetrator early in the investigation. Cleared him because he 'didn't fit our profile.'" She met James' eyes again. "I left the Bureau six months later. Couldn't trust my own judgment anymore."

"And the church?" he asked gently.

"Came later. Part of rebuilding my life. Finding purpose again." She straightened, visibly reclaiming her professional demeanor. "But that's not relevant to this investigation."

"I think it is," James countered. "It explains why you're here, why this case matters so personally, and why you understand Rebecca's pain so deeply."

Detective Collins didn't confirm or deny his assessment. Instead, she shifted the focus back to the case. "I notice you've been having private conversations with several church members. Anything I should know?"

It was James' turn to hesitate. Ethan's message weighed heavily on his conscience. His police training advocated for full disclosure to the lead investigator, while his pastoral instincts urged him to protect a potentially frightened young man's confidence. "There are... concerns about some financial questions at the church," he said finally, deciding on a middle ground. "Nothing substantial that I can see, but it might explain the source of that false news report."

The detective's eyes narrowed slightly. "Anything else?"

The moment stretched for what felt like an eternity between them, a test of trust on both sides. James made his decision. "Ethan texted me," he admitted, showing her the message on his phone. "He wants to meet. Alone. No police."

She read the message in its entirety without an expression and then looked up at him. "And were you planning to go?"

"I haven't decided yet," he replied honestly.

"This could be crucial evidence in a child abduction case," she pointed out, her tone neutral rather than accusatory. "Withholding it could be construed as an obstruction."

"I'm very well aware," he acknowledged. "That's why I'm showing it to you now."

She observed him for a moment longer before coming to a decision of her own. "I think you should go to the meeting."

That wasn't the response he expected. "You do?"

"Yes, but with proper precautions in place," she clarified. "We'll have officers positioned discreetly near the bridge. You'll wear a wire. If Ethan has information about Michael, we need to hear it right away. And he's more likely to talk to you than to anyone in law enforcement."

"And if he's involved in the kidnapping? Or what if it's a trap?"

"Then we'll be there to intervene," she said simply. "Sometimes, the best way to advance an investigation is to take a calculated risk."

James understood the logic, but concern still lingered. "Rebecca should know about the meeting."

Detective Collins nodded in agreement. "We'll tell her together. She deserves to be informed of anything that might lead to her son."

As if summoned by her name, Rebecca appeared at the lodge entrance. "The backpack is here," she announced, her voice tightly controlled.

They followed her inside to the command center, where an evidence technician had placed a child's blue backpack on a table covered with sterile paper. Rebecca approached slowly, as if the backpack might somehow disappear if she moved too quickly. "That's Michael's," she confirmed immediately. "I put those dinosaur patches on myself."

Detective Collins nodded to the technician, who carefully opened the backpack. Inside were items one would expect: a small water bottle, a child's sweatshirt, and a paperback book about salamanders. But nestled among these ordinary belongings was something unexpected—a sealed envelope with "Mom" written on it in childish handwriting.

Rebecca gasped as her hand flew to her mouth. "That's... Michael's writing."

"Ms. Chen," Detective Collins said softly, "we need to process this as evidence first. It may contain fingerprints or other trace elements that could help us find Michael."

Rebecca nodded, though it was obvious she had to exercise great restraint not to reach for the letter from her son.

The technician carefully removed the envelope with gloved hands and placed it in an evidence bag. "I'll expedite processing," he promised, feeling the emotional weight of the moment.

As he took the letter away, Rebecca remained fixated on the backpack, her fingers hovering just above its surface without touching. "He folded his sweatshirt," she observed, her voice breaking slightly. "I've been trying to teach him to fold his clothes instead of just stuffing them in his drawer."

The simple observation—a mother's pride in a small sign of her child's development—crystallized the human reality of their investigation more powerfully than any official report could have. Michael wasn't just a case number or a face on a missing poster; he was a little boy learning to fold his clothes, reading books about salamanders, and writing notes to his mother.

Detective Collins' phone buzzed, interrupting the poignant moment. She looked at it, her expression subtly changing. "The lab results on the blood from the truck are back," she announced. "It's not Michael's."

"Whose is it?" James asked.

"Martin Grayson's. And there's more. The state police found evidence of a struggle at the rest stop. It appears Martin may have been forcibly removed from his vehicle."

The implications hit hard. Their first suspect was now possibly another victim.

"Jesus. So, someone took both Michael and Martin?" Rebecca asked, struggling to make sense of this new development.

"Or," Detective Collins suggested carefully, "Martin took Michael, and then someone took Martin."

"Which brings us back to why," James said, thinking aloud. "If this isn't a typical predator abduction, what's the motive? What connects Michael, Martin, and possibly Ethan?"

The question remained unanswered as a deputy approached with a satellite phone. "Detective Collins, the FBI team at the rest stop needs to speak with you immediately. They've found something in the woods nearby." She took the call, stepping away for privacy.

James turned to Rebecca and said quietly, "There's something you should know." He explained Ethan's text and the details of the planned meeting.

She listened intently, her expression hardening with resolve. "I'm coming with you."

"Rebecca, it could be dangerous—"

"We're talking about my son," she interrupted. "And if Ethan knows anything about where he is, I need to be there."

Before James could respond, Detective Collins returned with a serious yet focused look. "They've found Martin," she announced. "Alive but injured. He's being airlifted to Regional Medical Center."

"And Michael?" Rebecca asked immediately.

"No sign of him at the location," the detective said carefully. "But Martin was conscious when they found him. He said something to the first responders before losing consciousness again." She paused, meeting Rebecca's eyes directly. "He said, 'The boy is alive. Church records. Look at the church records.'"

James and Rebecca exchanged bewildered glances. "What church records?" Rebecca asked. "What does that mean?"

"I don't know," James admitted. "But there's one person who might—Thomas. As church counsel, he oversees all our official documentation."

Detective Collins was already heading for the door. "Let's find Thomas. Now."

As they moved through the lodge, James felt the investigation shifting beneath them like tectonic plates shifting into new positions, preparing for the most remarkable moment of earthly destruction. If Martin wasn't a predator but possibly a protector—if the key to Michael's disappearance was in church records rather than in the portrait of a disturbed individual—then everything they had assumed about this case needed to be reconsidered.

And somewhere, in the back of his mind, Ethan's words echoed: *Not what you think. Need to talk. No police.*

Whatever truth was hidden in the church's past, it was about to surface—with potentially devastating consequences for everyone involved.

Chapter 7: Buried Secrets

T homas wasn't in the dining hall, his cabin, or answering his cell phone. His sudden disappearance—following Martin's cryptic message about church records—cast a long shadow of suspicion that Detective Collins wasn't quick to dismiss. "When was the last time anyone saw him?" she asked, her voice sharp with professional concern as they regrouped in the command center.

"About an hour ago," Eleanor reported. "He said he was going to his cabin to gather some documents for the statement to the press."

"Documents that he never delivered," James noted.

Rebecca stood slightly apart, her attention fixed on the evidence technician who had returned with Michael's letter. It had been carefully removed from the envelope, photographed, and placed in a clear protective sleeve. "We've processed it for prints and trace evidence," he explained. "You can read it now, but please handle only the protective cover."

With trembling hands, she accepted the document, her eyes immediately filling with tears as she took in her son's uneven handwriting. James moved to her side, offering silent support as she began to read aloud:

"Dear Mom, I'm okay. They say I have to stay hidden for a while, but I will come home soon. Don't be scared. The man says it's complicated, but it's to keep people safe. I remember to say my prayers every night like you taught me, and I have the cross you gave me to keep me calm. I love you a million billion. Michael."

She pressed the protected letter to her chest, a sob escaping despite her efforts to control it. "He's alive. He's really alive."

"This confirms it," Detective Collins said, her voice softening briefly before reverting to her analytical mode. "The note suggests multiple people involved—'they say.' And the reference to keeping people safe is significant. This doesn't fit a typical abduction profile."

"It sounds like Michael believes whatever reason he was given," James observed. "That he's being kept safe, not held against his will."

"We can't rule out manipulation. He may have been coerced into writing it," Detective Collins countered.

Rebecca shook her head firmly. "No. I know my son's writing—not just the handwriting, but the way he expresses himself. 'A million billion' is our thing, something we say to each other. This is genuinely from Michael, not dictated by someone else."

Detective Collins nodded, accepting Rebecca's assessment. "The reference to 'the man' is singular, which is interesting considering the earlier plural. Possibly Martin, since the backpack was found in his truck."

"But Martin said to check the church records," James reminded them. "What records would involve Michael or explain his kidnapping?"

Eleanor stepped forward hesitantly. "Thomas maintains the official church archives—historical documents, property deeds, and board minutes dating back decades. They're kept in the church office, but he has copies of many sensitive documents in his personal files."

"Which he might have brought to the retreat," James realized aloud.

"We need to search his cabin," Detective Collins decided. "Ms. Chen, would you be willing to sign a statement about Michael's letter? It will help us secure a warrant faster."

"Of course. Anything that helps find my son."

As Rebecca worked with an officer to complete her statement, Detective Collins pulled James aside. "The midnight meeting with Ethan is still on. But given these developments, I'm modifying the plan. We'll have more officers in position, and I'll be personally monitoring nearby."

"You think Thomas' disappearance and Ethan's message are connected," he surmised.

"I think," she replied carefully, "that there are too many coincidences accumulating. Martin told us to look at church records. Ethan was asking questions about church finances. Thomas has vanished with potentially relevant documents. And somehow, an eight-year-old boy is at the heart of it all."

James nodded grimly. "When can we search Thomas' cabin?"

"As soon as the warrant comes through. Meanwhile, I want to learn more about these church records. What might they contain that could relate to Michael's kidnapping?"

James considered this as memories of his seven years at First Community Church filtered through his mind. "Nothing obvious connects Michael to any historical church matter. The Chen family joined only two years ago, after David's death. They have no previous ties to the congregation or its history."

"Yet Martin specifically mentioned 'church records.' Were there any scandals in the church's past? Financial improprieties? Abuse allegations? Property disputes?"

Something clicked in James' memory at the mention of property. "The youth center," he said slowly. "Eleanor mentioned that the auditing committee—which Ethan was on—had questions about the contractor billing for the youth center renovations."

"Let me guess: Thomas was handling those questions?" the detective asked. "But how would that connect to Michael's kidnapping?"

"I have no idea, but the youth center property was donated by Lawrence Peterson's father, who recently passed away. And now, Lawrence is contesting the donation, claiming his father wasn't of sound mind."

Detective Collins' eyes sharpened with interest. "When exactly was this donation made?"

"I'm not sure. It predates my time as the Senior Pastor. Eleanor might know."

They went to find Eleanor, who was helping organize volunteers for the ongoing search efforts. When questioned about the Peterson donation, her brow furrowed in concentration. "That would have been... about 15 years ago, I believe. The senior Mr. Peterson donated the property after his wife died. It was a significant gift—prime commercial real estate that the church converted for the youth ministry."

"Fifteen years," Detective Collins repeated thoughtfully. "Around the same time as the child's disappearance in Washington state—the case where Martin was questioned."

The possible link lingered in the air, fragile and unsettling.

"Eleanor," James asked carefully, "what do you know about Martin's background before he came to Mount Hermon?"

"Very little," she admitted. "He was hired before my time as church secretary. But I do recall Thomas mentioning once that Martin came highly recommended by someone in church leadership."

"Who?" Detective Collins asked immediately.

"I'm sorry. I'm not certain," Eleanor replied, her expression apologetic. "But it might have been during Pastor Gregory's time. He was the Senior Pastor before you, James."

"And where is Pastor Gregory now?" the detective inquired.

"Retired to Florida five years ago," James answered. "But he and Thomas remained close. They served together for nearly 20 years."

Detective Collins made a note on her phone. "We'll need to contact him immediately."

Just then, an FBI agent approached. "Detective, the search warrant for Thomas' cabin has been authorized. The team is standing by."

"Let's go," she said, nodding to James to accompany her.

With each step toward the cabin, James felt the burden of suspicion growing heavier on his shoulders. Thomas had been a pillar of First Community Church long before he arrived—respected, trusted, and seemingly beyond reproach. The idea that he might be involved in anything leading to Michael's kidnapping was almost unthinkable.

Almost, but not entirely. James had learned over his years in law enforcement that respectability could sometimes serve as the perfect cover for darkness.

Thomas' cabin was one of the larger accommodations at the retreat center, reserved for senior staff and church leadership. The FBI team moved with practiced efficiency, documenting the scene before beginning their methodical search. Detective Collins and James observed from the doorway as the agents photographed and then carefully examined every nook and cranny.

"Phone and laptop are gone," one agent reported. "But we've found a briefcase in the closet. Locked."

"Secure it for processing," Detective Collins instructed. "Anything else noteworthy?"

"Travel items are still present. Toothbrush, medications in the bathroom. Appears to be a hasty departure rather than a planned absence," the agent informed.

James' gaze shifted to the small desk where several files were scattered, as if Thomas had been reviewing them when interrupted. From his position, he could see what looked like architectural drawings. "Those look like blueprints," he said, pointing at the desk.

The lead agent carefully photographed the desktop before examining the documents. "Plans for a building renovation," he confirmed. "Labeled 'Youth Center Phase Two.'"

"That's the project Ethan had questions about," James whispered to Detective Collins.

She nodded, her expression thoughtful. "Have those documents bagged and brought to the command center," she instructed the agent. "I want everything examined for potential connections to the Peterson donation and property."

As the search continued, James' phone vibrated with an incoming call. The screen displayed a number he didn't recognize. "Pastor Miller," he answered.

"Hi, James. It's Gregory," said the familiar voice of his predecessor. "I just got a concerning call from Thomas. He mentioned the FBI is investigating the church and something about Michael Chen's kidnapping. What's going on?"

James moved away from the cabin, signaling to Detective Collins to follow. "Pastor Gregory, I'm with Detective Collins from county law enforcement. When did Thomas call you?"

"About 20 minutes ago. He sounded agitated. Said there was a misunderstanding that needed to be cleared up." The retired pastor's voice carried genuine confusion. "He mentioned something about Martin and the church records but wasn't making much sense. Is Thomas in some kind of trouble?"

James put the call on speaker so Detective Collins could hear. "Pastor Gregory, you're on speakerphone now. We're trying to locate Thomas. Did he say where he was calling from?"

"No, he didn't, but I heard traffic in the background. Highway sounds, I think." There was a pause. "James, what's happening? Is Thomas involved in this child's disappearance?"

"We don't know yet," he answered honestly. "But we need to speak with him urgently. Martin Grayson was found injured, and he mentioned church records being connected to Michael's kidnapping."

Another pause, longer this time. "I was afraid this might happen someday," Gregory finally said, his voice suddenly heavy with what sounded like old regret.

"Afraid what exactly might happen?" Detective Collins interjected. "Pastor Gregory, if you have information relevant to this case, please share it now. A child's life may depend on it."

"It's... complicated," he replied hesitantly. "A matter from before your time, James. Something Thomas and I—and others on the board then—believed was resolved for the benefit of all involved."

"Sir," Detective Collins said, her tone sharpening with professional authority, "I need you to be specific. To what matter are you referring?"

"The Peterson donation," he admitted reluctantly. "There were... irregularities in how it came to the church. Conditions that weren't publicly disclosed."

James and Detective Collins exchanged confused looks. "What kind of conditions?" James pressed.

"I can't discuss this over the phone," Gregory replied evasively. "But if Thomas is involved in this situation, you need to understand he's always believed he was acting for the greater good—for the church's mission."

"Pastor Gregory," Detective Collins said firmly, "we are currently investigating a kidnapping. Any information you withhold could be considered obstruction of justice. I strongly advise you to share everything you know about the Peterson donation and its possible connection to Michael Chen—right now."

The silence stretched so long that James wondered if the connection had been lost.

Finally, Gregory spoke again, his voice resigned. "The donation came with a condition of silence. The property had... a history. Something Lawrence Peterson's father wanted buried, literally and figuratively. Martin was hired as part of that arrangement. To keep watch."

"Keep watch over what?" James demanded, a cold dread settling in his stomach.

"Not what. Who." Gregory's voice dropped nearly to a whisper. "A witness. A child who saw something he shouldn't have. The Petersons paid for his relocation and new identity. Martin was assigned to ensure the arrangement remained intact."

The implications hit James hard with sickening clarity. "The missing child from Washington state. The one Martin was questioned about 15 years ago. He wasn't missing at all."

"Correct. He was placed with a new family. Given a new life, far from Washington."

Detective Collins' expression had hardened like stone. "And now, Lawrence Peterson is contesting the property donation. Threatening to expose everything, right?"

"Thomas believed he was protecting the church," Gregory said defensively. "Protecting the boy, too. If the truth came out, the consequences would be devastating for everyone involved."

"Including Michael Chen?" James asked sharply. "How is he connected to any of this?"

Another long pause. "I don't know. Michael wasn't part of any arrangement I was aware of. But if Thomas is involved in his disappearance... God help him, he must believe he's serving some greater purpose."

Detective Collins had heard enough. "Pastor Gregory, I need you to come in for a formal statement immediately. This conversation has revealed a potential criminal conspiracy involving multiple parties."

"I understand. I'll drive up first thing tomorrow morning," he replied, sounding suddenly old and defeated. "James... I'm sorry. We thought we were doing the right thing. Helping a traumatized child start fresh, securing the church's future..."

"By burying the truth?" James asked, unable to mask the judgment in his voice. "Whatever happened 15 years ago is now endangering Michael Chen's life. That's the legacy of your silence and choice, Pastor Gregory."

After ending the call, James and Detective Collins stood in momentary silence, absorbing the implications of what they'd learned.

"Fifteen years of conspiracy to conceal a child's disappearance," Detective Collins finally said, her professional tone belied by the anger flashing in her eyes. "Multiple church leaders involved. Martin Grayson hired as a handler for the relocated child."

"And somehow, little Michael has become entangled in it," James added, struggling to make the connection. "But how? The Chen family has no ties to Washington state or to the Petersons."

Detective Collins was already heading toward the command center, James falling in step beside her. "We need to identify the child from Washington," she said. "Find out who they became, where they are now. That may be our link to Michael."

"And Thomas," James added. "If he took Michael to prevent Lawrence Peterson from exposing the church's secret…"

"Then Michael could be used as leverage, a bargaining chip," she finished the thought. "Or worse—a perceived loose end that needs to be eliminated."

The stark possibility hung between them as they reentered the command center. Rebecca looked up immediately, sensing the tension in their expressions. "What is it?" she asked. "What have you found out?"

Detective Collins hesitated, clearly considering how much to reveal. James stepped forward and gently placed a hand on Rebecca's shoulder. "We're uncovering a complex situation involving the church's past," he said carefully. "Something that may explain why Michael was taken. I promise you'll know everything once we confirm the details, but right now, speculation might do more harm than good."

Rebecca studied his face, then Detective Collins', her perceptiveness cutting through their careful words. "It's bad, isn't it? Whatever this church's secret is—it's something terrible."

"It appears to involve a cover-up from 15 years ago," Detective Collins offered, respecting Rebecca's right to some information. "We're working to understand how Michael fits into that picture."

Rebecca absorbed the news, her expression hardening with resolve rather than falling into despair. "I need to see Martin," she said suddenly. "If he knows where Michael is, I want to speak with him directly."

"Ms. Chen, Martin is in intensive care, under police guard. He's barely conscious," Detective Collins said.

"I don't care. He's the only person we've identified who definitely had contact with Michael after the kidnapping. I need to see him, speak to him if possible."

James saw the determination in her stance—the same fierce maternal resolve that had carried her through difficult hours. "She should go," he told Detective Collins. "And I'll go with her. You have the search for Thomas to organize and the investigation into the Peterson connection to handle."

"Okay. I'll arrange for a deputy to take you to the medical center. But Ms. Chen, you need to understand—Martin might not be able to communicate, and anything he says could be affected by his injuries and medication."

"I understand. But I have to try," Rebecca said firmly.

As arrangements were made for their hospital visit, James checked his watch—just past 8:30 p.m. The midnight meeting with Ethan still loomed ahead, but now with much greater significance, given what they'd learned about the church's buried secrets.

Eleanor approached him, looking worried. "James, the FBI agents found something else in Thomas' cabin. A file with financial records dating back 15 years. They've taken it for analysis, but I caught a glimpse of a page with my name on it."

"Your name?" he asked, surprised. "In what context?"

"A payment record," she replied, her voice hushed with confusion. "A substantial monthly sum labeled as 'administrative services.' But James, I never received such payments. My salary has always come through the regular church payroll, documented in my employment contract."

The implications sent another wave of unease through James. "Phantom payments using your name. Another layer of financial deception."

Eleanor nodded unhappily. "I've worked for First Community Church for 27 years. The thought that my name might have been used in some kind of—" she couldn't bring herself to say 'fraud' about her beloved church— "impropriety is devastating."

Before he could respond, Rebecca approached, ready to leave for the hospital. "The deputy is waiting," she informed him. "Detective Collins wants us back by 11:30 for the meeting preparations."

James nodded, gently resting a hand on Eleanor's shoulder. "We'll get to the bottom of this, Eleanor. Whatever happened, it wasn't your doing."

The drive to Regional Medical Center took 40 minutes, winding down from the mountain retreat through increasingly populated areas until they reached the outskirts of the city. The deputy remained largely silent, professional but reserved, while Rebecca stared out the window, clutching Michael's letter in its protective sleeve.

"He knew I would understand," she said softly, breaking the long silence. "His letter. He knew I would recognize his voice in it, knew he wasn't being forced."

"Michael is remarkably perceptive for his age, and he knows you better than anyone," James agreed.

Rebecca turned to look at him directly. "This church secret—you think Michael was taken to protect it? That someone believes my eight-year-old son is somehow a threat to whatever happened before he was even born?"

"It does seem that way, yes. However, the exact connection is still unclear."

"I keep thinking about that day at the retreat. Michael at the prayer stations. What could he have seen or heard that would make someone desperate enough to take him?"

"That's what we need to find out. And Martin may be our best chance at answers."

The hospital was a modern complex of glass and steel, its emergency entrance busy even at this late hour. The deputy escorted them efficiently through security procedures, his badge smoothing their path to the intensive care unit where Martin was being treated.

Another officer stood guard outside the room, verifying their IDs carefully before letting them in. Inside, the caretaker lay still amid a network of monitors and IV lines, his rugged face now pale and partly covered by an oxygen mask. Bandages were wrapped around his head, and his right arm was in a cast.

Rebecca approached the bed slowly, studying the man who was the last confirmed person to see her son. "Can he hear us?" she asked the nurse who was checking his vital signs.

"He's been drifting in and out of consciousness. The head injury is serious, but he has had lucid moments. Just keep your visit brief, please."

When the nurse exited, Rebecca finally moved closer to the bed. "Mr. Grayson," she said clearly, "I'm Rebecca Chen, Michael's mother. I need to know where my son is."

For several long minutes, there was no response. Then, Martin's eyelids fluttered open, revealing pain-clouded eyes that struggled to focus on Rebecca's face. "Safe," he managed, his voice barely audible through the oxygen mask. "Boy's safe."

"Where?" she pressed, leaning closer. "Where is Michael?"

Martin's eyes shifted to James, recognition dawning slowly. "Pastor," he rasped. "Tell her... not my idea... tried to protect..."

"Protect Michael from what?" James asked, moving to stand beside Rebecca.

"From them," Martin whispered. "Church... secrets. The boy... from Washington. He knows."

Rebecca's hand found James' arm, gripping it tightly. "Who knows? Michael? What does he know?"

Martin's eyes started to close again, the effort of speaking clearly draining his limited strength. "File... in cabin. Behind water heater. Everything... documented."

"Mr. Grayson," Rebecca said urgently, "please. Who has my son now?"

The caretaker's eyes opened once more, focusing with visible effort. "Ethan. Ethan took him... from me. Said... safer that way."

The name hit like a punch to the chest. James and Rebecca shared stunned looks as the implications sank in— Ethan didn't run out of fear or guilt; he had taken Michael from Martin, believing he could protect the boy better.

"Why?" James asked, leaning closer. "Why did Ethan take Michael from you?"

"Thomas," Martin managed, his voice fading. "Thomas wanted... silence. Permanent silence."

The cold meaning behind those words sent a chill through James, making the hairs on his arms stand on end. Before he could ask anything further, the monitors beside the bed began to signal distress, and medical staff rushed in, telling them to step back.

"BP dropping," a nurse announced. "He's crashing. You need to leave now." The deputy led them out of the room while a medical team surrounded Martin's bed.

Once in the hallway, Rebecca turned to James, her face a complex mix of hope and fear. "Ethan has Michael," she said, taking in the shock of the news. "And he's trying to protect him from Thomas?"

"It appears so," James replied, his mind racing to reconstruct the events of the past two days. "Martin must have taken Michael initially, perhaps believing the boy had uncovered something about the Washington case. Then Ethan intercepted them, assaulted Martin, and took Michael."

"And now, Ethan wants to meet you at midnight," Rebecca finished. "To explain or hopefully to arrange Michael's return."

"Or to seek help," James added, "if Thomas is, indeed, determined to ensure 'permanent silence' about whatever happened 15 years ago."

"We need to get back to the retreat center. Now. And I'm coming with you to that meeting, no matter what Detective Collins says."

James didn't argue, recognizing both the futility of trying to dissuade her and the validity of her presence at a meeting that might lead to her son's return. As they hurried back to the waiting deputy, his phone buzzed with an incoming call from

Detective Collins. "Pastor Miller," he answered, putting the call on speaker for Rebecca to hear.

"We've found something," she said abruptly. "The FBI team analyzing the blueprints from Thomas' cabin found writing on the back. It looks like it's in a child's handwriting. It says, 'The bones aren't supposed to be there.' Does that mean anything to you?"

James felt a cold weight settle in the pit of his stomach. "The youth center," he said slowly. "The renovation project. Michael must have seen something during his visits to the children's ministry."

"That's our theory as well. We're securing emergency authorization to search the youth center building now. And there's more. We've identified the missing boy from Washington state. His name was Christopher Scott. According to sealed court records, he witnessed a violent crime committed by Lawrence Peterson's brother. After recanting his testimony under pressure, he was relocated through a private agreement between the Petersons and certain parties at First Community Church."

"And now, he's an adult," James surmised, "who could expose everything if Lawrence Peterson's legal challenge proceeds."

"Exactly. We're working to locate him under his new identity."

"Detective," James said urgently, "we've spoken with Martin. He's confirmed that Ethan has Michael. He took the boy from Martin to protect him from Thomas, who apparently wants to ensure 'permanent silence' about whatever is buried at the youth center."

There was a moment of silence as Detective Collins absorbed this new information. "That changes the dynamics of your midnight meeting significantly," she said finally. "If Ethan is protecting Michael rather than harming him, we need to proceed with extreme caution. He may flee if he sees any sign of law enforcement."

"I agree," James said. "And Rebecca insists on being present. Given what we now know, I think that's appropriate."

After a brief hesitation, Detective Collins concurred. "Her presence might actually reassure Ethan of our intentions. But we'll need to modify your approach. Minimal visible presence, maximum surveillance from a distance."

"We're heading back now. We should arrive in enough time to prepare."

As they finished the call and rushed to the deputy's vehicle, James felt the burden of 15 years of secrets weighing on him. Whatever was buried at the youth center—literal or figurative—had now endangered an innocent child and threatened to shatter the foundation of the church community he had promised to shepherd.

And somewhere in the darkness, Thomas was undoubtedly plotting his next move—a man who believed himself righteous even as he considered the unthinkable to keep his secrets.

The race to midnight had begun, with Michael Chen's life hanging in the balance between those who wanted to reveal the truth and those who aimed to bury it forever at any cost.

Chapter 8: Crisis of Faith

The drive back to Mount Hermon had a surreal feel. The deputy's silent focus on the winding mountain roads stood out against the chaotic thoughts rushing through Rebecca's mind. Michael's letter was in her hands—solid proof of her son's ongoing existence in a world that felt more and more disconnected from everything she believed to be true. "He's with Ethan," she said, breaking the heavy silence. "All this time, we've been searching, and he's been with our youth pastor."

James nodded, his expression troubled as he looked out at the dark landscape. "A youth pastor who apparently believed taking Michael was the only way to protect him."

"From Thomas," she added, the name now carrying a weight of menace that seemed impossible to reconcile with the dignified church deacon she had known for two years. "A church elder willing to ensure 'permanent silence' about whatever secrets they've been hiding."

The implications hung between them, too disturbing to fully articulate. What kind of Christian leaders conceal crimes, relocate witnesses, and threaten a child's life to maintain their deception?

"I keep thinking about Sunday services," she continued, her voice hollow with disillusionment. "Thomas passing the communion tray, praying over the offering, quoting Scripture about truth and integrity—all while knowing what he'd helped conceal."

James didn't respond right away, and Rebecca realized he was probably dealing with his own crisis—a pastor discovering that the church he was called to lead was built on secrets and lies from before his time.

"How much of it was real?" she asked quietly. "The worship, the fellowship, the promises of God's presence in our lives? Was it all just... a performance?"

James turned to her then, his expression somber but resolute. "The failure of church leaders doesn't negate God's reality, Rebecca. Humans have always been capable of profound hypocrisy, of using holy things to conceal unholy actions. That's why Scripture repeatedly warns about wolves in sheep's clothing."

"Wolves who led the flock," she replied bitterly. "Wolves who decided what was righteousness and what was sin. Wolves who told us to trust them as God's representatives."

"Not all of them," James countered gently. "Eleanor has served faithfully for decades. Most of the congregation has no idea about any of this. Their faith, their worship—that's genuine."

Rebecca clenched Michael's letter more tightly. "You know what terrifies me the most? That Michael is witnessing all of this. Learning that the same people who taught him Bible stories and led him in prayers were capable of... whatever is buried at that youth center." Her voice faltered slightly. "How do I help him understand that when I'm struggling to understand it myself?"

After a thoughtful pause, James replied, "With honesty. Acknowledge that followers of Christ can fail badly and that churches can hide darkness along with light. But also, show him that true faith keeps confronting that darkness, rather than denying or hiding it."

Rebecca absorbed this, finding a thread of truth to hold onto amid her spiritual vertigo. "Like Ethan," she said slowly. "Whatever his methods, he chose to protect Michael rather than preserve the church's secrets."

"Yes. And like you, refusing to surrender hope despite everything that's happened."

The deputy's radio crackled to life with an update from the command center. They were 20 minutes away from the retreat, and Detective Collins was requesting their immediate presence upon arrival.

The drive continued in quiet contemplation, the weight of the upcoming confrontation weighing heavily on them as they neared the midnight meeting that could finally reunite Rebecca with her son.

****

The command center buzzed with focused activity as they arrived. Detective Collins greeted them at the entrance, her expression carefully controlled but with an unmistakable sense of urgency. "We have developments," she announced, leading them to a private conference room. "The FBI team at the youth center has discovered a sealed section beneath the building's foundation. It looks like an old basement that was intentionally hidden during renovations 15 years ago."

"The bones," James said grimly.

Detective Collins nodded. "Ground-penetrating radar shows anomalies consistent with human remains. They're proceeding carefully to preserve evidence, but preliminary findings suggest we're dealing with a homicide cover-up."

Rebecca pressed a hand to her mouth, the horror of it momentarily overwhelming her composure. "And Michael somehow discovered this?"

"We believe so," the detective confirmed. "Children's ministry activities were being held in temporary trailers beside the main building during the renovation. Michael attended regularly, according to church records. He may have wandered into an area he shouldn't have, seen construction plans, or overheard something he wasn't meant to."

"The blueprints in Thomas' cabin," James realized. "Michael could have seen those same plans at the youth center and noticed the discrepancy with the actual construction."

Detective Collins picked up a tablet, swiping to display a child's drawing. "This was found in Michael's Sunday School folder at the church office. Drawn three weeks ago."

The crayon drawing depicted a simple building labeled "God's House" with stick figures playing outside. But beneath the structure, drawn in an ominous black crayon, was a box containing what looked like a person lying down.

"He knew," Rebecca whispered, staring at her son's drawing. "Somehow, he knew what was hidden there."

"Children often express through art what they can't articulate verbally," Detective Collins noted. "Michael may not have fully understood what he was drawing, but it clearly represents something he observed or intuited."

"And Thomas recognized the significance when he saw it," James added, the pieces fitting together with sickening clarity. "Realized Michael had somehow discovered their secret."

"Which brings us to our current situation," Detective Collins continued, checking her watch. "The meeting with Ethan is in 90 minutes. We've adjusted our approach based on what we now know." She displayed a map of the Riverbrook Bridge area on the tablet. "We'll have officers positioned here, here, and here—far enough back to stay undetected but close enough to respond if needed. You'll both be wearing discreet transmitters so we can monitor the conversation. The goal is to persuade Ethan that we're allies in protecting Michael, not threats."

"He'll be suspicious," James warned, "especially if he believes Thomas has influence with local authorities."

"That's why Ms. Chen's presence is crucial. A mother's concern for her child is universal and unambiguous. Ethan will recognize that her only priority is Michael's safety."

Rebecca nodded, her determination hardening her features. "I'll do whatever it takes. But there's something else we need to consider: if Thomas realizes we're meeting Ethan, he might try to intercept us."

"We've considered that," Detective Collins assured her. "We have officers monitoring all approaches to the bridge, and we'll take an alternative route to the meeting point. However, there's another issue." She hesitated briefly. "We've identified the relocated witness from Washington state. Christopher Scott, who is now living under the name Peter Sanderson."

The mention of the name nearly took James' breath away. "Sanderson? As in—"

"Jake and Tyler Sanderson's father," Detective Collins confirmed. "He was given a new identity, eventually married, and had children. The boys who were playing with Michael just before his disappearance are the sons of the very witness whose protection may have fueled this entire conspiracy."

Rebecca's eyes widened with shock. "I know that family. Michael has playdates with those boys. Their father is... quiet. Keeps to himself, mostly. I never would have imagined—"

"He's been living with this secret for 15 years," Detective Collins said. "And now, with Lawrence Peterson contesting the property donation, the legal proceedings threaten to expose everything—his true identity, the crime he witnessed, and the arrangement that gave him a new life."

"And potentially endanger his family," James added, understanding dawning. "If the people involved in the original crime discovered his whereabouts—"

"Exactly," the detective agreed. "We're trying to locate Peter now. He dropped his wife and sons at home after the retreat was disrupted by Michael's disappearance, but he hasn't been seen since. His wife reported him missing this morning."

Another disappearance linked to the growing web of secrets. Was Peter Sanderson hiding, worried about being exposed? Or had Thomas also made sure he stayed silent?

"We need to focus on the immediate priority," Detective Collins said, steering them back to the upcoming meeting. "Securing Michael's safety. FBI agents will continue investigating the youth center site and searching for both Thomas and Peter."

As they prepared for the midnight rendezvous— receiving their transmitters, reviewing the approach plan, and being briefed on emergency protocols—Rebecca found a quiet moment to step outside the command center. The night air was cool and clear. The stars above Mount Hermon shone brilliantly in their remote serenity, untouched by the human drama unfolding below. She closed her eyes, clutching Michael's letter to her chest, and did something she hadn't done since his disappearance: she prayed in complete privacy, with no witness to her spiritual struggle.

"God," she whispered into the darkness, "I don't understand any of this. How Your church could harbor such secrets, how Your people could justify such deception. I'm angry—at Thomas, at Pastor Gregory, at everyone who chose institution over integrity. And I'm angry at You for allowing this to happen, for not protecting my son from their conspiracy." She paused, letting her tears fall freely now. "But Michael still believes. Even in captivity, he says his prayers each night. He trusts that You see him in the darkness. And I need to believe that, too—not because the church taught me, but because I've experienced Your presence in my life, independent of any human authority." Her voice strengthened with resolute conviction. "So, I'm asking, not as a proper church member reciting correct prayers, but as a desperate mother: help me find my son tonight. Guide Ethan to trust us. Stop Thomas from silencing anyone else. Expose whatever evil has been buried in Your name. And if Your justice comes through flawed human vessels like me, like James, like Detective Collins—then use us, even in our imperfection. In Jesus' name I pray, Amen."

With the prayer finished, Rebecca opened her eyes to see James standing at a respectable distance, waiting to escort her to the vehicle that would take them to Riverbrook Bridge. He didn't comment on her tear-streaked face or private moment of prayer. Instead, he simply offered his arm in silent support.

"I'm ready," she said, and meant it in ways that transcended the immediate mission. She was ready to face whatever truth awaited at the bridge... whatever consequences came from uncovering long-buried secrets... whatever rebuilding of faith might be required in the aftermath.

****

Riverbrook Bridge spanned a deep gorge about five miles from the retreat center. Built in the 1930s, its stone arches and narrow passage were deemed inadequate for modern traffic, and a newer bridge was constructed nearby, leaving this historic structure primarily for pedestrians and occasional maintenance vehicles.

At 11:45 p.m., James parked their unmarked vehicle at the designated spot: a small turnout a quarter of a mile from the bridge. From here, they would approach on foot, reducing the chance of startling Ethan with the sound of a car arriving.

"Transmitters check," came Detective Collins' voice through their earpieces. She was monitoring from a surveillance position with clear sightlines to the bridge. "We have both your signals. Remember, speak clearly but naturally. If you feel threatened at any time, use the phrase 'time to pray,' and we'll move in immediately."

"Understood," James confirmed, adjusting the small microphone concealed beneath his collar. "Any sign of activity at the bridge yet?"

"Negative. Perimeter is secure with no sign of Thomas in the vicinity."

James turned to Rebecca, who stood silhouetted against the moonlit landscape, her expression resolute. "Ready?" She nodded, and together they started walking toward the bridge, following the old access road that gleamed faintly in the moonlight. The night was eerily quiet except for their footsteps and the distant splash of the flowing creek far below the gorge.

As they neared the bridge, James felt the burden of his dual duties weighing on him—pastor to a fractured congregation, de facto investigator in a case that had unveiled corruption at his church's core. The familiar comfort of clear moral boundaries had been broken, replaced by uncertainties he couldn't have foreseen when he had planned this spiritual retreat just weeks earlier.

"Someone's there," Rebecca whispered, pointing to a shadowy figure at the midpoint of the bridge.

James squinted, recognizing Ethan's lanky figure even in the dim moonlight. The young pastor stood alone, hands deeply shoved in his pockets, nervously shifting his weight from foot to foot. "He's alone," James confirmed for Detective Collins' benefit. "Proceeding to make contact." They moved quickly and purposefully toward the bridge, making no effort to conceal their approach.

When they were about 20 yards away, Ethan's head snapped up, and his posture instantly tensed. "Pastor James," he called, his voice tense with anxiety. "You were supposed to come alone."

"I brought Michael's mother," James replied calmly, continuing forward at a steady pace. "She deserves to hear whatever you have to tell me."

Ethan hesitated, clearly weighing this unexpected development. "Are there police with you?" he demanded. "Because if there are—"

"No police," Rebecca interjected, her voice carrying clearly across the remaining distance. "Just a mother who wants her son back. Please, Ethan. If you know where Michael is, if you're protecting him—I need to see him."

Something in her direct appeal seemed to reach through Ethan's suspicion. He relaxed fractionally, though his eyes continued scanning the surroundings warily. "You don't understand how dangerous this is," he said as they reached the midpoint of the bridge. "Thomas has connections everywhere. The sheriff's department, the county prosecutor's office—he's their legal counsel for certain matters. That's why I couldn't go to the authorities."

"Is that why you took Michael from Martin?" James asked carefully.

Ethan's surprise was obvious. "How did you—" He paused, reconsidering where the conversation might head next. "Yes. Martin had good intentions, but he didn't understand the full extent of what Thomas was capable of. After Michael found those old blueprints and noticed the discrepancy with the actual construction..."

"Martin told us there's evidence in his cabin," Rebecca said. "Behind the water heater. He said everything is documented."

Ethan nodded grimly. "Fifteen years of records. Martin was hired to monitor Peter Sanderson—Christopher Scott back then—to ensure he maintained his new identity and stayed quiet about what he had witnessed."

"The murder at the youth center property," James surmised.

"Lawrence Peterson's brother murdered a business rival during an argument," Ethan confirmed. "Christopher was delivering newspapers and saw it all. The Petersons had influence and connections. They arranged a deal with certain church leaders—a property donation in exchange for helping to relocate the witness and establish a new identity."

"And the body was concealed during the youth center construction," James concluded, the horrific picture now complete. "Buried in the foundation, hidden from the authorities."

Ethan nodded miserably. "I only discovered it recently when reviewing the contractor invoices for the current renovation. Materials that made no sense. Specialized concrete work in areas that shouldn't have needed it. Then I found old files in Thomas' office while looking for the original contracts."

"Ethan, where is Michael now?" Rebecca asked, cutting through the explanations to focus on the questions that mattered most to her. "Is he safe? When can I see him?"

Ethan hesitated, his internal conflict visible even through the darkness. "He's safe. Hidden where Thomas won't think to look. But I can't just bring him back—not while Thomas is still free and desperate to cover his involvement."

"Ethan," James said gently, "Martin is in intensive care. The FBI is excavating the youth center site as we speak. Thomas' role in the cover-up is being exposed regardless of what happens with Michael. The best thing you can do now is return him to his mother."

"The FBI?" Ethan's eyes widened with shock. "They're actually digging? Thomas said they'd never get authorization without more evidence, that he could block any investigation through legal channels."

"Thomas overestimated his influence," James replied. "And underestimated how rapidly things would unravel once Michael disappeared. Please, Ethan. Tell us where Michael is."

Ethan was about to give in when headlights suddenly appeared at the far end of the bridge. A vehicle was racing toward them. "It's him," Ethan hissed, panic flaring in his eyes. "Thomas! He must have followed you!"

James turned to see a dark SUV screech to a stop at the bridge entrance, its headlights casting a harsh white light. A tall figure stepped out from the driver's side. Even from a distance, James recognized Thomas' distinctive silhouette.

"Detective Collins," James said urgently into his concealed microphone. "Thomas has arrived at the bridge. Situation potentially volatile."

"Units moving in," came the immediate response in his earpiece. "Stall him, if possible. Keep everyone talking."

Thomas was advancing toward them now. Something was clutched in his right hand that James couldn't clearly identify in the backlighting from the vehicle. "James! Rebecca!" he called, his voice carrying a forced friendliness that did nothing to hide the tension beneath. "And Ethan, too. What a fortunate coincidence."

"Stay back, Thomas," Ethan warned, stepping protectively in front of Rebecca. "I know what you did. What you've been hiding all these years."

Thomas kept his steady approach, now close enough for James to see his face—the familiar features set in a pained expression of reasonableness. "Ethan, you've misunderstood everything. Jumped to conclusions based on incomplete information." His gaze turned to James. "I've been trying to reach you, to clarify the situation properly."

"The 'situation' where you helped cover up a murder?" James challenged, positioning himself slightly to Ethan's right, creating distance between them that would force Thomas to divide his attention. "Where you threatened a child to protect that secret?"

Thomas flinched slightly, but his voice remained steady. "It's more complicated than that. Everything we did was aimed at protecting the church and securing its future. The Petersons' donation funded ministries that have helped thousands of people over the years."

"Including the ministry where you buried a body," Rebecca said, her voice vibrating with controlled fury. "Where my son innocently played, never knowing what lay beneath his feet."

Thomas' expression hardened. "Rebecca, I understand you're upset about Michael. But he's fine—just temporarily removed from a volatile situation until certain legal matters can be resolved."

"Removed?!" Rebecca echoed in disbelief. "He's an eight-year-old boy, not an inconvenient file! You kidnapped my son!" she yelled.

"I ensured his safety," Thomas countered, taking another step forward. James could now see that he held a small revolver at his side—not pointing it directly at them, but its presence was unmistakably threatening. "When Michael found those blueprints and started asking questions and drawing pictures... It was a temporary measure until we could contain the situation."

"By silencing Martin?" Ethan accused. "Is that why he's in intensive care? Another 'temporary measure'?"

A flash of genuine surprise crossed Thomas' face. "Martin's alive? I was told the accident was... conclusive."

The casual mention of what had obviously been an attempted murder sent a shiver through James. This was not the Thomas Webb he knew as a colleague and church elder—or maybe it was, and he had just never seen past the carefully maintained façade of Christian propriety.

"Thomas," James said evenly, "law enforcement is on the way. The FBI is excavating the youth center. There's no containing this situation anymore. The best thing you can do now is put down that weapon and tell us where Michael is."

Thomas' expression shifted subtly, calculation replacing the veneer of reasonableness. "I don't think so, James. Michael is my insurance policy. Once I'm safely away, arrangements will be made for his return."

"He's lying," Ethan said flatly. "Thomas, tell them what you told me yesterday—about loose ends that needed permanent tying."

Rebecca gasped, and James felt a cold certainty settle in his stomach. Thomas had never intended to return Michael alive—not once the boy had seen evidence of the church's darkest secret.

"Where is Peter Sanderson?" James asked suddenly, trying to change tactics. "Christopher Scott. The witness you helped relocate 15 years ago. Is he just another 'loose end' you've tied up?"

Something flickered in Thomas' eyes—surprise again, then quick recalculation. "Peter made his choice," he said carefully. "When Lawrence started challenging the property donation, threatening to expose everything. Peter understood what was at stake."

"You mean he refused to cooperate," James translated. "Wouldn't help you silence Michael to protect your secret."

"He was ungrateful," Thomas snapped, the first real crack in his composed demeanor. "Fifteen years of a new life, a family, safety—all provided through our intervention. And when the church needed his loyalty in return, he balked at the necessary measures."

"'Necessary measures,'" Rebecca repeated, her voice thick with disgust. "Is that what you tell yourself to sleep at night? That kidnapping a child, attacking an old man, and possibly murdering the witness you claimed to protect—these were 'necessary measures'?"

Thomas's grip visibly tightened around the gun, and James tensed, ready to move if the weapon was raised toward Rebecca. "You can't understand," Thomas insisted, an edge of desperation entering his voice. "The scandal would have destroyed the church. Not just reputations, but the ministries, the outreach programs, and everything we've built. Thousands of lives positively impacted, souls saved, communities transformed. All of it at risk because of one regrettable incident 15 years ago."

"An incident where someone was murdered," James pointed out. "Where church leaders conspired to conceal evidence, obstruct justice, and use donated funds to effectively bribe a witness."

"We did what was necessary," Thomas emphasized, the justification sounding increasingly hollow even to his own ears, judging by the uncertainty now creeping into his expression. "For the greater good."

"There is no 'greater good' that justifies evil means," James said firmly. "That's not Christianity, Thomas. That's not even faith. That's the opposite of everything we're called to stand for as believers."

Thomas' face contorted with sudden anger. "Don't lecture me about faith, James! You've been here for what? Seven years? I've given my life to the church. Decades of service, of sacrifice. Everything I did was to protect God's work!"

"No," Rebecca said with quiet certainty. "What you've done was protect yourself, your reputation, and your position of authority. Don't blaspheme God by claiming He needed you to kidnap my son, bury a body in cement, and silence witnesses in His name!"

Something she said seemed to penetrate Thomas' defensive rationalizations, hitting at a deeper truth he had long suppressed. For a brief moment, uncertainty flashed across his face—a glimpse of the man he might have been before decades of compromise and justification had warped his moral compass. That moment passed, replaced by a cold resolve. He raised the revolver slightly, not quite aiming at them but clearly ready to do so. "I need you to come with me," he said. "All of you. We're going to get Michael, and then we'll negotiate with the authorities. No one needs to get hurt... if you cooperate."

"Thomas Webb!" Detective Collins' voice roared from behind, amplified by a bullhorn. "This is Detective Sarah Collins. You are surrounded by law enforcement. Drop your weapon and put your hands on your head."

Thomas stiffened, his head snapping around to see patrol cars now blocking both ends of the bridge, officers in tactical positions with weapons drawn. For a terrible second, James feared he might raise the gun and provoke a confrontation that would likely end in bloodshed. Instead, Thomas' shoulders sagged—not in surrender but in grim determination. He turned back to them, his expression now eerily calm. "It was never about the money," he said, addressing James directly. "I need you to understand that. It was about protecting the mission and ministry. Everything I did, I believed was for God's Kingdom." Before anyone could respond, Thomas turned and ran—not toward the officers blocking the bridge but toward the stone railing that separated them from the gorge below.

"Thomas, don't!" James shouted, lunging forward even as he recognized the futility of the gesture.

Thomas Webb, an Elder of First Community Church, a respected attorney, and the secret guardian of a 15-year conspiracy, vaulted over the railing in a single, fluid movement. His body disappeared into the darkness, the splash reaching them seconds later as a distant, final punctuation to his desperate flight from justice.

Officers converged on the bridge, securing the scene with practiced efficiency. Detective Collins reached them moments later, her expression grim but focused. "Are you all okay?" she asked, scanning them for injuries.

James nodded numbly, the shock of Thomas' apparent suicide momentarily robbing him of words.

Rebecca, however, turned immediately to Ethan. "Please," she said, her voice cracking. "Take me to my son. Now."

Ethan stared at the railing where Thomas had vanished, his face pale with shock. After a moment, he seemed to compose himself, nodding with renewed determination. "He's with Peter Sanderson's wife," he revealed. "At their house. Thomas would never have thought of looking there. He figured Peter would have taken his family and fled when the investigation began."

"Mrs. Sanderson is caring for Michael?" Detective Collins clarified, already speaking into her radio to redirect units to the Sanderson residence.

"Yes," Ethan confirmed. "After I took Michael from Martin, I needed a safe place, somewhere Thomas wouldn't suspect. Mrs. Sanderson understood immediately when I explained the situation. She's been living with this secret hanging over her family for years, never knowing the full story until recently."

"And Peter?" James asked. "Thomas implied something happened to him."

Ethan shook his head. "Honestly, I don't know. He disappeared yesterday after taking his wife and sons home from the retreat. Said he had to 'take care of some things.' Mrs. Sanderson is terrified that Thomas may have... eliminated him."

Detective Collins grew visibly upset. "We'll need statements from all of you, but first, let's get to the Sanderson home. Ms. Chen has waited long enough to see her son."

As they were escorted to a patrol car, Rebecca found herself in the strange position of feeling both vindicated and devastated. The truth had come out, just as she prayed it would. Thomas could no longer threaten her son, but the cost—in broken trust, shattered faith, and now a human life—felt almost too heavy to bear. "What happens to the church now?" she asked James quietly as they settled into the backseat. "How does a community recover from something like this?"

James looked out at the nighttime scene, the flashing lights of emergency vehicles reflecting his inner turmoil. "Honestly? I don't know. But recovery always begins with truth, however painful. Then comes repentance, restoration, and rebuilding." He turned to her, his face serious but resolute. "The Christian church as a whole has endured corruption and human failure since it began. That's why our faith ultimately depends on Christ, not on fallible leaders."

Rebecca nodded, drawing some measure of comfort from his words. As the patrol car pulled away from Riverbrook Bridge, heading toward what she prayed would be a reunion with her son, she found herself whispering the words from Psalm 23:4 that had sustained generations through their darkest valleys:

"Though I walk through the valley of the shadow of death, I will fear no evil..."

The valley had, indeed, been dark, shadowed by deception and death. But somewhere ahead, beyond this crisis of faith that had shaken her to the core, Rebecca believed that light still awaited her—beginning with holding her son in her arms once more.

Chapter 9: The Judgment

D awn was breaking over the mountains when Rebecca finally cradled her son in her arms again. The Sanderson home—a modest two-story in a peaceful suburb—became the setting of a reunion that brought tears to even the most experienced law enforcement officers present.

"Mom!" Michael cried as he burst from an upstairs bedroom, having been gently woken by Mrs. Sanderson with the news of his mother's arrival. He flew down the stairs and across the living room, launching himself into Rebecca's waiting embrace with such force that she staggered backward.

"Michael!" she cried, her voice a mix of prayer and gratitude as she held him tightly against her chest, inhaling the familiar scent of his hair and feeling the solid presence of his small body against her. "Oh, my sweet boy."

For several minutes, they remained locked in that embrace—Michael's face buried against his mother's shoulder, Rebecca gently rocking as tears flowed freely down her face. The room around them faded into the background, with officers and investigators becoming mere shadows during this sacred moment of healing. When they finally pulled apart slightly, Rebecca cupped her son's face in her hands, examining him for any signs of trauma or harm. His eyes were clear, though tinged with fatigue, but they still held the resilience and spark that defined her extraordinary child. "Are you hurt?" she asked, running her hands over his arms and shoulders, as if to reassure herself of his wholeness.

"I'm okay, Mom," he reassured her with a maturity that both comforted and broke her heart. "Mrs. Sanderson made sure I was safe. She even found books for me about reptiles from Jake and Tyler's collection."

Rebecca glanced gratefully toward the tired-looking woman hovering nearby. Renee Sanderson appeared to have aged years in the past few days, her face drawn with worry, not just for Michael but also for her own missing husband. "Thank you," she said simply, words insufficient to express her true feelings.

Renee nodded, understanding passing between the two mothers. "He's a remarkable boy. He's been so brave through all of this."

Detective Collins approached carefully, kneeling to Michael's eye level. "Hello, Michael. I'm Detective Collins. I've been helping your mom find you."

He regarded her solemnly. "Are you going to arrest the bad men who were fighting over me?" he asked.

The innocent question carried profound implications, and Detective Collins exchanged a quick glance with James, who stood nearby. "We're going to make sure that the responsible people face justice," she assured him. "Can you tell me a little about what happened? Who took you from the retreat?"

Michael looked at his mother, who gave an encouraging nod before he answered. "Mr. Grayson, the mountain man. He said I was in danger because of what I found."

"What did you find, Michael?" James asked gently.

"The wrongness," he replied, his brow furrowing as he searched for words to express concepts beyond his years. "In the building plans at church. There was a room beneath that wasn't supposed to be there, but I saw it on the old papers. And then I heard Mr. Webb talking to someone about making sure no one ever found what was hidden there."

"You're very smart and very observant," Detective Collins said, carefully keeping a conversational tone despite the importance of Michael's revelation. "What happened after Mr. Grayson took you?"

"We camped in the woods. He said we had to wait until he could talk to someone important who would know what to do. But then Mr. Parker found us." Michael's expression brightened slightly. "He said Mr. Grayson was trying to help but didn't understand how dangerous Mr. Webb was. So, he brought me to Mrs. Sanderson instead."

"Did anyone hurt you, Michael?" His mother asked the question she had been dreading but needed answered.

Michael shook his head firmly. "No. Mr. Grayson was kind of scary-looking but nice. He gave me his jacket when it was cold. And Mr. Parker made sure I could write you a letter so you wouldn't worry too much."

Rebecca closed her eyes briefly in relief, silently thanking God for this mercy amid the horror. Her son had been taken but not harmed, frightened but not traumatized beyond recovery.

"Michael," Detective Collins continued gently, "did you ever see Mr. Sanderson—Jake and Tyler's dad—during the time you were here?"

A sad shadow crossed Michael's face. "No. Mrs. Sanderson was crying about him. She said he went to fix things but didn't come back."

Renee made a small, painful sound from where she stood. James moved to her side, offering quiet support as Detective Collins continued her careful questioning of Michael.

"Last question for now," the detective promised. "Did you ever hear anyone mention where Mr. Sanderson might have gone?"

Michael frowned as he concentrated. "Mr. Parker and Mrs. Sanderson were talking when they thought I was asleep. Mr. Parker said something about Mr. Sanderson going to 'confront his past' and that it was dangerous. Mrs. Sanderson said he took something with him for protection."

Renee stepped forward. "Peter took his father's old hunting rifle," she admitted quietly. "He said... he said he wouldn't let them silence another witness. That he was tired of running from what happened in Washington."

Detective Collins' expression sharpened as she looked at Renee. "Mrs. Sanderson, where exactly did your husband go?"

"I don't know for certain," she replied, her voice trembling. "But he mentioned the Peterson estate. Said Lawrence wasn't the one he was worried about; it was the brother, Richard. The one who..." She couldn't finish the sentence.

"The one who committed the original murder," James finished grimly. "The crime Peter witnessed as a kid."

Detective Collins immediately got on the radio, ordering units to the Peterson estate, requesting updates on the youth center excavation, and coordinating the expanding investigation.

Amid the activity, Rebecca focused solely on her son, drawing him back into her embrace. "You're safe now," she whispered against his hair. "No one will ever take you away from me again."

Michael nestled against her, but his next words revealed how much he had taken in of the adult drama around him. "Mom? Is our church bad? Because Mr. Webb did bad things?"

The question pierced Rebecca's heart with its innocent profundity. How could she explain the complex reality of human institutions and of faith corrupted by fear and power to an eight-year-old?

James approached, kneeling beside them. "Michael, do you remember our lesson about King David?"

Michael nodded. "Yes. He was a good king who did a very bad thing."

"That's right. The Bible doesn't hide that God's people fail or sin. Churches are made up of humans, and humans sometimes make terrible mistakes or do wrong things. But that doesn't make God or faith bad."

"Even when it's church leaders doing the bad things?" Michael persisted, his perceptiveness startling for someone so young.

"Especially then," James said soberly. "Jesus had very strong words for leaders who abused their positions. He said they would face stricter judgment."

Michael considered this with the seriousness of a theologian. "Like Mr. Webb jumping off the bridge? Was that his judgment?"

Rebecca and James exchanged alarmed glances, wondering how Michael knew about Thomas' apparent suicide. Renee stepped forward, looking distressed. "He overheard a phone call," she explained. "One of the officers called to update me about an hour ago. I didn't know Michael was listening."

James addressed Michael directly, choosing honesty tempered with pastoral care. "Mr. Webb made a desperate choice rather than face the consequences of his actions. But God's judgment is more complete than that. It brings truth to light, justice to victims, and eventually, healing to communities."

"Like what's happening now?"

"Yes," James confirmed, once again impressed by the boy's insight. "Exactly like what's happening now."

Detective Collins rejoined them, her expression grim but composed. "We need to move everyone to a secure location. There's been a development at the Peterson estate."

"What's happened?" James asked, rising to his feet.

"Reports of gunfire," she replied, keeping her voice low enough that Michael wouldn't hear. "And we've confirmed that Richard Peterson returned from Europe three days ago, coinciding with the start of the retreat and just before Michael's disappearance."

The implications were clear: Peter had possibly faced his childhood traumatizer—the man whose crime changed the entire course of his life. Whether that confrontation had ended in further violence was still uncertain.

"Where are we going?" Rebecca asked, maintaining a calm façade for Michael's sake while her mind raced with this new information.

"The FBI has secured rooms at a hotel downtown," Detective Collins explained. "Renee and her sons will be coming as well. We're worried that Richard Peterson might have associates willing to tie up loose ends, especially now that the youth center excavation is getting media attention."

"Headlines?" James echoed, surprised at how fast the news had spread.

Detective Collins nodded grimly. "Local stations broke the story an hour ago. Social media is amplifying it. We've got reporters gathering outside First Community Church, and congregants are arriving confused and distressed. Sheriff Larson has deputies maintaining order, but the situation is volatile."

"I should be there," James said immediately, feeling the weight of his pastoral responsibility despite his own shock and fatigue. "My congregation needs guidance through this crisis."

"Pastor Miller, you might be at risk," Detective Collins warned. "You've played a key role in exposing this conspiracy. Until we know exactly who's involved beyond Thomas Webb, you should stay protected along with the others."

"Respectfully, detective, my duty is to my congregation, especially in times of crisis. I can't hide in a hotel while they face this trauma alone."

She studied him for a moment, then nodded reluctantly. "I'll arrange a security detail. But first, we need to get Ms. Chen and Michael safely to the hotel."

Rebecca listened to their exchange while holding Michael close. "James should go to the church," she agreed softly. "Those people will be lost and frightened. They need their pastor now more than ever."

As arrangements were made to transport everyone securely, an FBI agent approached with a satellite phone. "Detective Collins? There's a call from the team at the youth center. They've completed the initial excavation."

The room fell silent as she took the call, her body language revealing nothing until she finished the conversation and turned to face them with her shoulders slumped. "They've recovered human remains. An adult male, with the estimated time of death consistent with the period 15 years ago, when the youth center was built. Physical evidence supports the theory that this was the business rival Richard Peterson allegedly murdered."

"Allegedly no longer," James replied. "Not with a body found exactly where Peter said it would be."

"But there's something else," Detective Collins continued, her brow furrowed. "They found a second set of remains. Partial skeletal remains of a child, estimated age between eight and ten years old, were buried deeper in the foundation."

Rebecca instinctively covered Michael's ears, though he was now distracted by Jake and Tyler, who had emerged sleepily from upstairs.

"A... child?" James repeated, the horror evident in his voice. "That wasn't part of the story Peter shared."

"No, it wasn't," the detective agreed. "Which means there might be aspects of this case even Peter doesn't know about—or has chosen not to reveal."

The implications were staggering—a darker, more sinister secret beneath what they had already uncovered. Had Richard Peterson killed a child witness, too? Had church leaders conspired to cover up not just one murder, but two? Who was this child?

"I need to speak with Peter," Renee said suddenly, her voice stronger than it had been previously. "If there's another victim—a child—he would have told me. Whatever happened at that property 15 years ago, Peter wouldn't have hidden something that horrific from me."

"If we can find him," Detective Collins reminded her. "And if he's still alive."

That somber assessment lingered in the air as they prepared to leave the Sanderson home, the weight of judgment—both human and divine—bearing down on them with renewed seriousness.

****

First Community Church presented a surreal scene when James arrived two hours later, escorted by law enforcement. News vans lined the street, and reporters gathered at the police barricade around the perimeter. Beyond them, church members huddled in confused, anxious groups across the parking lot, many in tears, some arguing heatedly, a few standing in silent prayer.

At the heart of this chaos was the youth center—a modern building next to the main sanctuary, now surrounded by forensic tents and a variety of FBI vehicles. The excavation site was out of public view, but everyone knew what had been discovered beneath the cheerful structure where children played, unaware of the grim secret hidden below.

As James stepped out of the patrol car, a wave of recognition spread through the crowd. Voices called his name— some pleading for reassurance, others demanding answers, and a few hostile with accusations. He understood them all. These people were experiencing the spiritual equivalent of an earthquake, as the foundation of their faith community suddenly appeared unstable, hiding horrors they could never have imagined.

Eleanor pushed through the crowd to reach him. Her elderly face was marked with grief, but her posture remained steady. "James, thank God you're here. Everyone's in shock. No one knows what to believe."

"Is Michael safe?" asked a woman clutching a Bible to her chest like a shield. "We've been praying nonstop."

"Michael is safe," James confirmed, raising his voice to reach as many people as possible. "He's with his mother, unharmed. I've spoken with him myself."

A murmur of relief swept through the crowd, but was soon replaced by more pressing questions.

"Is it true? About Thomas?"

"Are there really bodies under the youth center?"

"How could this happen in our church?"

"Did you know about this, Pastor?"

That last question, delivered with accusatory force by a man James recognized as a relatively new member, struck at his deepest fear—that his congregation might believe he had been complicit in the cover-up.

"I learned about this conspiracy at the same time you are learning now," he replied, addressing not just the questioner but the entire gathering. "Thomas Webb and certain former church leaders made decisions 15 years ago that were not only criminal but counter to everything our faith represents. They chose institutional protection over truth, self-preservation over justice." He paused to gather his thoughts, aware that his words would need to address not just the facts of the case but also the spiritual crisis it had sparked. "I know many of you are feeling betrayed, confused, angry—perhaps even questioning your faith. Those are natural, even necessary responses to this revelation. The Bible never asks us to deny reality or suppress righteous anger at injustice. What happened here was evil, perpetrated and concealed by people who claimed to serve God while violating His most fundamental commands."

A tense silence had fallen over the crowd, each person digesting James' words through their own lens of shock and disorientation.

He continued. "In the coming days, we will learn more about what happened, who was involved, and what justice requires. As your pastor, I commit to complete transparency. No more secrets, no more protecting the institution at the expense of the truth."

"But how do we move forward?" Eleanor asked, voicing the question on everyone's mind. "How does a church recover from something like this?"

James had been asking himself the same questions since the horrific truth began to emerge. Now, facing his wounded congregation, he offered not empty words but a way forward—difficult, uncertain, but guided by faith that went beyond human failure.

He inhaled deeply before speaking once more. "We begin by acknowledging the full truth, no matter how painful. We offer genuine repentance—not just words, but actions that show our commitment to justice and healing. We support the victims and their families with everything we have. And we rebuild, not the same structures of power and secrecy that allowed this tragedy, but something more authentic, humbler, and more in line with Christ's example." He looked around at the faces before him, some nodding cautiously in agreement, others still struggling with shock, and a few turning away in disillusionment. "This church is not Thomas Webb or Pastor Gregory or any other individual leader. It is all of us, together, choosing how to respond to this moment of judgment. Because, make no mistake, this is judgment. Not the final judgment of God, but a moment when hidden things are exposed, when we are called to account for who we have been and challenged to become what we should be."

Before he could continue, a commotion near the police barricade caught everyone's attention. A police cruiser had arrived, and out of it stepped a familiar figure: Martin Grayson. His head was bandaged, his arm in a cast, his face pale with pain but showing resolve. He spoke urgently to Detective Collins, who had apparently escorted him from the hospital.

James moved toward them, the congregation temporarily forgotten as he recognized the importance of Martin's presence. As he approached, he could hear the caretaker's persistent voice.

"I'm telling you, it's not what everyone thinks! The second body—the child—is not connected to Richard Peterson. It's much older, from before the property was even purchased."

Detective Collins noticed James and signaled him to come over. "Pastor Miller, Mr. Grayson has information relevant to the investigation. He was insistent on coming here directly from the hospital."

"The files in my cabin," Martin said, turning to James with feverish intensity. "Did you find them? The complete documentation?"

"FBI agents searched and secured your cabin, but I don't know what specifically they found yet," James replied.

Martin's expression tightened with frustration. "Then you don't have the full picture yet. The child's remains were discovered during the initial excavation for the youth center. Richard Peterson didn't kill that child. The remains were already there, buried decades earlier, according to the forensic assessment at the time."

"Still, the church leadership concealed this discovery," Detective Collins surmised. "Instead of reporting it to the authorities."

"Yes," Martin confirmed. "It was the first secret, the start of the compromise. Thomas convinced everyone that reporting the discovery would delay construction indefinitely and cost the church the Peterson donation. So, they documented it privately and kept building."

"Then Richard Peterson killed his business rival on the property," James continued, piecing together the expanding narrative. "And a second body was buried in the same foundation."

"Creating a deeper secret, a stronger bond of complicity," Detective Collins added grimly. "Each decision makes the next compromise easier to justify."

Martin nodded wearily. "I was hired after everything that happened. My job was to monitor Christopher Scott—Peter Sanderson—and ensure he maintained his new identity. I knew about the business rival's murder, but I only found out about the child's remains later, from documentation Thomas had supposedly destroyed."

"And Michael discovered evidence of this," James said, the final pieces clicking into place. "Not just the murder Peter witnessed, but the church's double deception."

"He found the old blueprints showing the original excavation sites," Martin confirmed. "Started asking innocent questions that terrified Thomas. When I realized what was happening—that Thomas was planning to 'permanently resolve' the situation—I took Michael. Thought I could protect him until I gathered enough evidence to expose everything safely."

"But Ethan intercepted you," Detective Collins stated.

"Yes. He had his own suspicions and was investigating the financial irregularities in the youth center renovation. When he found me with Michael, he convinced me that Thomas had too much influence with local authorities and could block any investigation. Said the boy would be safer elsewhere while he gathered more evidence."

A clamor of voices from the police barricade interrupted their conversation. James turned to see officers responding to a vehicle that had arrived at high speed, skidding to a halt at the perimeter. Two men stepped out of it. One, he immediately recognized as Peter Sanderson, looking haggard and desperate. The other was an older man in expensive clothes, hands raised in apparent surrender.

"That's Richard Peterson," Martin gasped in shock. "And Peter's got him at gunpoint."

Detective Collins was already moving toward the developing situation, signaling for backup while giving orders to secure the perimeter and evacuate civilians. James followed instinctively, aware that his presence might help diffuse the volatile confrontation.

As they approached, they could hear Peter's voice, charged with decades of suppressed emotions. "Everyone needs to hear the truth! No more secrets! No more protection for murderers!"

Despite the hunting rifle aimed at his back, Richard remained calm. "Put the gun down, Christopher. You've made your point. I'm here to turn myself in, as agreed."

"After 15 years!" Peter yelled, the name 'Christopher' clearly fueling deeper anger. "After you killed that man, threatened me, and made me give up my entire identity! After your family used money and influence to cover up the truth!"

Officers had established a cautious perimeter, weapons ready but not directly engaged, understanding the delicate nature of the situation. Detective Collins approached slowly, hands visible. "Mr. Sanderson, I'm Detective Collins. We've been looking for you. I understand you have a lot to say, and we want to hear it all. But first, I need you to lower the weapon so that no one gets hurt."

Peter's gaze darted to her, then to James as he recognized the pastor. "They found the bodies," he said, not a question but a statement. "Tell me they found them."

"Yes," James confirmed. "Both of them. The truth is coming out, Peter. Richard will face justice for what he did."

"Both?" Peter's brow furrowed in a moment of confusion, the rifle dipping slightly. "What do you mean 'both'?"

James exchanged a quick glance with Detective Collins, realizing that Martin was correct: Peter didn't know about the child's remains. "The forensic team found two sets of remains," James explained carefully. "The man Richard killed 15 years ago, and... another victim. A child, buried earlier."

Peter's face showed shock, then devastating understanding as he looked at Richard. "There was another body? A child? And you built over that, too?"

For the first time, Richard's composed façade cracked. "I didn't know about that until after construction began," he insisted, an edge of desperation entering his voice. "Thomas Webb informed me privately, used it as leverage. Said if I ever revealed what happened with Jameson, the church would expose that earlier discovery and implicate my family, since we'd owned the land for generations."

"Mutually assured destruction," Detective Collins observed coldly. "Each party holding damaging information against the other."

"Who was the child?" Peter demanded from Richard as he raised the rifle again. "Another victim you silenced? Another witness to your family's crimes?"

"I don't know!" Richard's composure completely shattered, revealing the terrified man beneath the wealthy exterior. "The remains predate our ownership of the property! Some earlier tragedy no one knew about until the excavation!"

James took a cautious step forward, sensing that this moment was teetering on the edge between violence and resolution. "Peter," he said softly, "Michael is safe. Your wife and sons are safe. The truth is finally coming out. Don't add to this tragedy with more violence."

Something in James' words—maybe the mention of his family—pierced Peter's rage. The rifle lowered slightly again as conflict flickered across his face.

"He's right," Detective Collins added. "Richard Peterson will face justice through the courts. Your testimony will be crucial to that process. Your family needs you whole, not torn apart by a moment of vengeance."

Peter's gaze flicked between them, then settled on Richard, whose arrogance was completely gone, replaced by a frightened older man facing the fallout of long-hidden crimes. "Fifteen years of my life," Peter said, voice trembling. "A new name, a made-up history, constant fear of being found out. Do you have any idea what that's like? To live a lie every single day, even with the people you love most?"

"No," Richard admitted quietly. "No, I don't. And I can't undo what my actions caused. But I'm here now, surrendering to the authorities, prepared to confess everything."

The revelation that Richard had come voluntarily and that Peter had somehow convinced his former traumatizer to surrender shifted the dynamic even more toward resolution.

"He contacted me," Peter explained, seeming to read the question in their expressions. "After Thomas called him about Michael discovering the blueprints. Said he was tired of living with the guilt, that he wanted to make amends before more innocent people were hurt."

"So, you didn't abduct him at gunpoint?" Detective Collins clarified.

"No," Richard confirmed. "I reached out to Christopher—Peter—when Thomas' behavior became increasingly erratic. I feared he might take desperate measures to preserve our mutual secret."

"Which he did, by kidnapping Michael Chen," James observed grimly.

Peter finally lowered the rifle completely, the fight draining from him as the complex truth surfaced. "I never wanted anything related to this to touch my family. I thought I'd buried Christopher Scott completely and built a new life as

Peter Sanderson. Then Lawrence contested the property donation, investigators began examining old records, and suddenly, the past wasn't just the past anymore."

Detective Collins moved forward cautiously, securing the rifle and then signaling for officers to take Richard into custody. As they led the older man away, he turned back briefly and said, "I'm sorry for everything my actions set in motion, Peter."

Peter watched him leave, 15 years of trauma visible in his expression. "Is it really over?" he asked quietly.

"The cover-up is," Detective Collins replied honestly. "The investigation, the legal proceedings—those are just beginning. But the truth is finally emerging, so yes, it's over."

Peter nodded, exhaustion overtaking him now that the confrontation had ended. "My family? Renee and the boys?"

"Safe," James assured him. "Being taken to a secure location where you can join them once we've taken your statement."

As Peter was led to a patrol car for official questioning, James once again noticed the crowd watching the scene from beyond the barricade. Their expressions ranged from shock to grief to a strange, emerging relief—the relief that comes when a long-festering wound is finally lanced, painful but essential for healing to begin.

Eleanor came up to him with a tear-streaked face. "All these years," she whispered. "Serving alongside Thomas, never suspecting..."

"You couldn't have known," he assured her. "None of us could."

"Some suspected, you know," she countered, her integrity intact despite the years. "There were whispers, questions about the Peterson donation, about certain financial arrangements. But we trusted our leaders, believing they would never compromise on core ethical issues." She shook her head sadly. "We made them gods, James. Elevated them beyond accountability."

Her assessment struck him as profoundly accurate. The root of the tragedy wasn't just individual moral failures but a church culture that had made leaders unquestionable, prioritizing institutional success over transparency and truth.

"That changes now," he promised her. "If I remain as pastor, that changes fundamentally."

"If?" she echoed, alarmed. "James, the congregation needs you now more than ever. You're the one person untainted by this scandal."

He smiled sadly. "But I represent a system that enabled it. The same hierarchical structure, the same concentration of authority that Thomas exploited." Before Eleanor could respond, his phone rang. It was Detective Collins, who had moved to consult with FBI agents near the youth center.

"Pastor Miller, we have a situation developing at the hotel where Ms. Chen and Michael are staying. Security protocols have been triggered. We need you there immediately."

"What's happened?" he demanded, cold fear displacing his philosophical contemplations.

"Ethan has arrived, demanding to speak with Michael. He's agitated, claiming there's more to the story than anyone realizes. Something about evidence still hidden at the retreat center."

"I'm on the way," he promised, already moving toward the patrol car that had brought him to the church.

"One more thing," Detective Collins added, her voice tense. "Ethan insists he's not acting alone. He says he's working with someone from within the congregation—someone who's been gathering evidence against Thomas for years."

"Who?" he asked, though a terrible suspicion had already formed.

"He won't say. Only that it's someone 'above suspicion' who recognized evil at the church's core long before anyone else."

As James ended the call and hurried to the waiting vehicle, the weight of judgment pressed down with renewed force. The revelations weren't complete, the full accounting not yet rendered. Someone else had been moving behind the scenes—someone from within his congregation, watching, waiting, and gathering evidence against Thomas Webb and his conspirators.

Someone whose identity would soon be revealed, bringing with it yet another layer of this complex tragedy that had begun with a child's innocent discovery of blueprints that didn't match the building where he played.

The reckoning continued, and James Miller—pastor, former detective, and shepherd of a fractured flock—could only pray for wisdom as he raced toward this next confrontation... aware that divine judgment often worked through human instruments, revealing truth regardless of the cost to institutions or individuals who had placed themselves above accountability.

Chapter 10: The Monumental Revelation

The drive to the hotel where Rebecca and Michael were being protected passed in tense silence as James' mind raced through the possibilities. Who within his congregation had been working alongside Ethan, gathering evidence against Thomas? Someone "above suspicion"—the phrase itself suggesting a person of irreproachable standing, trusted implicitly by the church community.

The list of potential candidates was disturbingly short.

"What exactly did Ethan say when he arrived?" James asked the officer driving him, seeking any additional details that might illuminate the situation.

"I wasn't there, sir," the young deputy replied. "But Detective Collins reported he was agitated, insisting on speaking with Michael. Said something about 'the final piece of evidence' being at risk of destruction now that Thomas Webb was gone."

James nodded, considering this. Whatever Ethan believed Michael had seen—beyond the blueprints already uncovered—it was significant enough to risk approaching a secure location under FBI protection. Was it desperation? Or confidence that his mysterious ally offered some form of protection?

The hotel came into view—an upscale establishment on the outskirts of the city, its circular drive now occupied by patrol cars and unmarked federal vehicles. As James exited the cruiser, Detective Collins emerged from the lobby to meet him. "Ethan's in a conference room under guard," she reported briskly. "He's refusing to speak with anyone except you and Michael. Says you'll understand once you hear what he has to say."

"And Rebecca? Michael?"

"Secure in their suite with FBI protection. Ms. Chen is understandably reluctant to involve Michael in additional questioning after everything he's been through."

"As she should be," James agreed. "Let me talk to Ethan first. Try to find out what he thinks is so urgent without involving Michael right away."

Detective Collins nodded in agreement. "We'll monitor the conversation remotely. If Ethan reveals information requiring immediate action, we'll respond accordingly."

She led him through the hotel's elegant lobby, now turned into an impromptu command center, with law enforcement personnel strategically stationed throughout. The conference room where Ethan waited was on the second floor, accessible via a service corridor to ensure privacy. Two agents stood outside the door, acknowledging Detective Collins with professional nods before allowing both inside.

Ethan sat alone at a long table, his normally cheerful face tired and strained. When he saw James, he stood quickly. "Pastor James," he said, relief clear in his voice. "Thank God. They need to listen to me. There's still evidence at the retreat center that Thomas didn't manage to destroy."

"Evidence of what exactly?" James asked, taking a seat across from Ethan while Detective Collins stayed standing, remaining silent and watchful.

"The full extent of the conspiracy," Ethan replied, leaning forward intently. "Not just the Peterson murder and cover-up, but also the financial web Thomas created to buy silence and control anyone who might threaten exposure." He glanced nervously at Detective Collins before continuing. "There are records hidden in the retreat center chapel, beneath the pulpit platform. A failsafe my... 'associate' has been maintaining for years."

"This associate," James pressed gently, "is someone from the congregation?"

Ethan hesitated, conflict evident in his expression. "Someone who recognized the corruption at the heart of the church long before anyone else. Someone who positioned themselves to gather evidence while remaining beyond suspicion."

"Why not come forward sooner?" Detective Collins interjected. "If this person has been collecting evidence for years, why wait until a child was kidnapped to act?"

"They tried!" Ethan insisted, his voice rising with frustration. "Subtle approaches at first. Anonymous tips to regulatory agencies and carefully planned questions during board meetings. But Thomas was too powerful, too connected. His legal expertise let him block every attempt at official investigations."

James studied the young pastor's face, observing the true distress along with the conviction behind his words. "Ethan, why involve Michael? How does an eight-year-old boy fit into this years-long conspiracy?"

"He wasn't supposed to be involved," Ethan admitted, guilt flashing across his features. "But when he found those blueprints and started asking innocent questions, Thomas panicked. The timing couldn't have been worse. Lawrence Peterson was contesting the property donation. The planned renovation could potentially expose the remains. Suddenly, this child stumbled onto evidence that connected everything."

"So, Martin took him," James summarized. "To protect him from Thomas."

"Yes, but it wasn't just Martin acting alone. He was directed to remove Michael from the retreat by someone he trusted—someone who recognized the danger Thomas posed more clearly than Martin himself did."

The pieces were beginning to align in James' mind. A disturbing pattern was coming into focus. "Your associate," he said slowly. "The person who's been gathering evidence, who directed Martin to take Michael... who then directed you to take the boy from Martin..."

Ethan nodded, a strange mix of pride and concern on his face. "Someone who's been hidden in plain sight for years. Someone whose position granted them access to documents, conversations, and evidence that no one else could get without suspicion."

A cold certainty settled in James' stomach as the final piece clicked into place. There was only one person at First Community Church who met all these criteria—who had unrestricted access to confidential information, whose presence in any church office or meeting would never be questioned, and whose decades of service placed them above suspicion. "Eleanor," he said quietly, the revelation landing with the weight of absolute truth. "It's Eleanor."

Ethan's expression confirmed it before he nodded. "For 27 years, she witnessed the church's darkest secrets while being treated as little more than furniture in the room. Board members, pastors, even Thomas—they spoke freely in front of her, as if her position made her invisible, irrelevant."

"But she was documenting everything," James realized aloud, memories reshuffling with this new understanding. Eleanor's meticulous attention to detail, her encyclopedic knowledge of church history, her subtle, probing questions about Thomas' handling of various matters... all taking on new significance now.

"She tried to work within the system at first," Ethan continued. "Brought concerns to Pastor Gregory, then to you when you arrived. But the evidence was circumstantial, the accusations against someone universally respected in the congregation."

"So, she recruited you," Detective Collins surmised, joining the conversation. "A younger staff member with access to different areas of church life."

Ethan nodded. "Two years ago. She noticed me questioning some financial irregularities in the youth ministry budget. Instead of shutting me down, she subtly guided me toward a deeper investigation. Eventually, she revealed what she suspected about Thomas, the Peterson donation, and the buried secrets."

James felt a complex mix of emotions: admiration for Eleanor's determined pursuit of truth, hurt that she hadn't trusted him fully, and a sobering recognition that her caution had been justified, given how deeply the corruption had infiltrated the church's leadership. "Where is Eleanor now?" he asked, suddenly alert to her absence from this unfolding revelation.

"That's what I've been trying to tell you," Ethan said urgently. "She went to the retreat center this morning—said

145

there were records Thomas hadn't found, evidence that would complete the documentation of the conspiracy. She was supposed to check in hours ago but hasn't responded to any of my messages."

James exchanged an alarmed look with Detective Collins, who was already reaching for her radio. "We need to send units to the retreat center immediately," she ordered. "Potential missing person situation, possibly in danger."

"I need to go, too," James insisted as he stood. "I know the retreat center well, including areas Eleanor might use to hide evidence."

"We'll take my vehicle," Detective Collins stated. "Mr. Parker will stay here under protection until we verify if his information is accurate."

"The chapel platform," Ethan called as they moved toward the door. "Look beneath the center panel. James—" his voice dropped, heavy with significance, "remember Jael."

The biblical reference stopped James in his tracks. Jael was the woman from the Book of Judges who appeared to offer sanctuary to the enemy general Sisera, only to drive a peg through his temple while he slept, becoming an unlikely instrument of divine judgment. A chill ran down his spine as he realized the implication. "Ethan, are you saying Eleanor might—"

"What I'm saying is that she's been waiting 15 years for justice. Gathering evidence, yes, but also preparing for the possibility that human justice systems might fail. Thomas' suicide denied her that resolution."

"But Richard Peterson is in custody," Detective Collins pointed out.

146

"Richard was only part of the conspiracy," Ethan countered. "There were others involved in the cover-up, in keeping the secret all these years. Eleanor has a list—names, dates, financial transactions."

"And she's gone to secure that evidence," James concluded, already moving toward the door hastily. "Before anyone else can destroy it."

As they hurried through the hotel, James turned to Detective Collins. "I need to speak with Rebecca before we leave. Just briefly." The detective nodded her understanding, redirecting their path toward the secure suite where Rebecca and Michael were staying.

When Rebecca responded to the security team's announcement, her expression changed from wariness to relief upon seeing James. "What's happening?" she asked right away, keeping her voice quiet. Michael could be seen in the background of the suite, absorbed in a book about reptiles, momentarily distracted from the ongoing drama around him.

"We've identified Eleanor as the person who's been working behind the scenes," James explained quickly. "She apparently directed both Martin and Ethan in their efforts to protect Michael from Thomas."

Rebecca's eyes widened with surprise. "Eleanor? But she's—"

"Been at the church longer than anyone," James completed. "In a position to observe and document everything without raising suspicion."

"But why wouldn't she come forward sooner?"

"She tried, in her own way," James replied. "But without solid evidence against respected church leaders, who would believe the elderly church secretary? Now she's gone to retrieve final documentation from the retreat center, and we're worried she might be in danger—or possibly planning something beyond legal justice."

Rebecca absorbed this with remarkable composure, her perspective clearly transformed by recent events. "What do you need from me?"

"Just to know if Michael mentioned anything about Eleanor during his time at the retreat. Any interaction that seemed significant in retrospect."

Rebecca thought for a moment, then softly called to her son. "Michael, can you come here for a moment? Pastor James has a question for you."

Michael approached cautiously, his young face serious but resilient. "Is it about Miss Eleanor?" he asked, surprising them all with his perceptiveness.

"Yes," James confirmed, kneeling to the boy's eye level. "Did you talk to her during the retreat?"

Michael nodded. "At the prayer station. She helped me make the card for mom, but then..." He paused, brow furrowing in concentration. "Then she asked me about the drawing I made at Sunday School. The one with the secret room under the building."

"What did she say about your drawing?"

"She said I was very observant, that I saw things other people missed. She asked me if I'd seen anything else interesting at church recently." Michael's expression grew troubled. "When I told her about the papers in Mr. Webb's office showing the hidden room, she got very quiet. Then she said I should be careful who I talked to about it."

"Did she seem angry? Scared?"

Michael considered this with the direct perception of a child. "Not angry. More like... when mom gets really determined about something important. She told me I was brave like David facing Goliath, but that sometimes, wisdom means knowing when to be quiet until the right time."

The biblical reference—Eleanor's second, James observed—had clear implications in hindsight. She had recognized the danger Michael's discovery posed to him and immediately understood its importance to her years-long documentation of the conspiracy. "Thank you, Michael," he said, managing a reassuring smile despite his growing worry. "You've been very helpful."

As Michael returned to his book, Rebecca followed them to the door. "Please find her," she said quietly. "Whatever Eleanor has done, she tried to protect my son when others would have silenced him forever."

With this sobering charge, James and Detective Collins departed, racing toward the retreat center where Eleanor Simmons—the seemingly unassuming secretary who had witnessed decades of corruption while meticulously documenting it all—had gone to retrieve her final evidence against those who had betrayed the church she had served faithfully for 27 years.

****

Mount Hermon Retreat Center appeared abandoned as they approached, the grounds eerily silent after the chaos of recent days. The FBI had processed the primary crime scenes and released the property, though warning tape still cordoned off certain areas. Eleanor's small blue Buick was parked near the main lodge, confirming she was there.

"The chapel is on the north side," James directed as they exited Detective Collins' vehicle. "It's the small building with a bell tower."

They approached cautiously. Detective Collins drew her weapon as a precaution while reporting their location over her radio. The chapel door stood slightly ajar, a slice of dim light visible within.

"Eleanor?" James called out, pushing the door open wider. "It's James Miller. Are you here?"

Silence greeted them, broken only by the faint creaking of the old building settling in the afternoon heat. The chapel was a simple, beautiful space—wooden pews facing a raised platform with a handcrafted pulpit at its center. Stained-glass windows cast colorful patterns onto the floor, although their cheerful hues did little to dispel the tension hanging in the air.

"The platform," James murmured, moving toward the raised area at the front of the chapel. "Ethan said beneath the center panel."

Detective Collins followed, her trained gaze scanning the area for any signs of disturbance or danger. Together, they examined the wooden platform, discovering a barely visible seam in the central section.

"There's an access panel here," James confirmed, his fingers tracing the outline. "Probably designed for running cables or audio equipment." He located a recessed handle and lifted, revealing a small storage space beneath the platform. Inside lay a waterproof document case, sealed and labeled with the simple inscription: 'The Truth – E.S.' "Eleanor's documentation," James said, reaching for the case.

"Don't touch it yet," Detective Collins cautioned. "This is evidence in an ongoing investigation."

A voice from the chapel entrance froze them both in place. "It's more than evidence. It's 15 years of waiting for justice."

They turned to see Eleanor standing in the doorway, her slight figure silhouetted against the afternoon light. She held something in her hand that James initially couldn't recognize—until she stepped forward, and he realized it was the antique letter opener she always keeps on her desk at the church office. Its brass handle and long, slender blade caught the light from the stained-glass windows, turning an ordinary office tool into something more threatening.

"Eleanor," James said carefully, turning to face her. "We've been worried about you."

"No need," she replied, her voice surprisingly calm. "I'm exactly where I need to be, finishing what I started 15 years ago when I first suspected Thomas was hiding something terrible." She moved further into the chapel, her gaze fixed on the document case still visible in the storage space.

Detective Collins maintained her professional composure, though her hand remained near her weapon. "Ms. Simmons," she said evenly, "we understand you've been gathering evidence against Thomas Webb and others involved in the conspiracy. That documentation could be crucial to securing justice through proper legal channels."

A small, sad smile crossed Eleanor's face. "Hmph. Proper legal channels. Yes, I tried those. Anonymous tips to regulatory agencies, carefully worded concerns to board members, even a letter to the district attorney after I first found evidence of financial irregularities connected to the Peterson donation."

Her voice then hardened. "All buried, dismissed, or diverted before they could become formal investigations. Thomas was very efficient at protecting his secrets."

"Thomas is gone now," James pointed out gently. "Richard Peterson is in custody. The truth about what happened at the youth center is being revealed."

"Not the whole truth," Eleanor countered, taking another step forward. "Not the full extent of the conspiracy, the other church leaders involved, and the financial web Thomas created to ensure silence." She gestured toward the document case. "That contains everything—names, dates, transactions. The complete accounting."

"Then let us use it," James urged. "Let the proper authorities—"

"The proper authorities had their chance!" Eleanor interrupted, a lifetime of deference finally absent from her tone. "For 15 years, I watched Thomas twist Scriptures to justify evil, to silence questioning, to maintain power. For 15 years, I listened while he quoted verses about unity and loyalty to pressure others into complicity." Her hand tightened around the letter opener. "No more."

The biblical reference Ethan had mentioned—Jael—suddenly took on urgent significance. James studied Eleanor's face, recognizing the calm determination of someone who had moved beyond conventional justice to something more primal, more absolute. "Eleanor," he said carefully, "what are you planning to do with that evidence? With that letter opener?"

Her smile was terrifying in its serenity. "Proverbs 28:13 – 'Whoever conceals their sins does not prosper, but the one who confesses and renounces them finds mercy.'"

"You've given people a chance to confess," James interpreted, taking a cautious step toward her. "Is that why you gathered all this evidence? To force confessions before judgment?"

"Precisely. I compiled the documentation, then approached each person involved privately. Gave them the opportunity to come clean, to seek redemption through honest confession."

"And if they refused?" Detective Collins asked, though her tone suggested she already knew the answer.

Eleanor's gaze shifted to the letter opener in her hand, studying it with academic interest. "Thomas wasn't the only one who could quote Scripture selectively. Hebrews 10:30 – 'For we know Him who said, 'It is mine to avenge; I will repay.''"

"You're not talking about divine justice," James said, the horrifying truth crystallizing. "You're talking about carrying out that judgment yourself."

"Only when necessary," Eleanor clarified, as if discussing a minor administrative matter. "Thomas denied me that resolution. But there are others who refused confession, who chose continued concealment over repentance."

"Who, Eleanor?" James pressed, desperately seeking to understand the full extent of her intentions. "Who else was involved that hasn't been identified yet?"

Eleanor's expression hardened, decades of accumulated grievance finally finding voice. "Pastor Gregory, for one. He presents himself as the reluctant participant, dragged into Thomas' scheme against his better judgment. But he was an eager collaborator, seeing the Peterson donation as his legacy, his crowning achievement as Senior Pastor."

"Pastor Gregory is being questioned by the FBI," Detective Collins informed her. "His involvement will be fully investigated."

"Questioning isn't the same as confession," Eleanor countered. "True repentance requires a public acknowledgment of sin, complete transparency about one's actions." She took a small step forward, her normally gentle demeanor transformed by righteous certainty. "There are seven individuals beyond Thomas who were directly involved in concealing the murder and manipulating church funds to ensure silence. Seven. I've approached each one. Three confessed privately and provided sworn statements, which are included in that documentation. One died of natural causes five years ago. Thomas chose suicide rather than face justice."

The math was chilling. "That leaves two unaccounted for," James said contemplatively. "Besides Pastor Gregory."

Eleanor nodded like a teacher acknowledging a student's correct answer. "Lawrence Peterson's attorney, who structured the donation to conceal its true purpose. And—" her voice caught momentarily before hardening again, "the current head of the church finance committee, who has continued to manage the shadow accounts that Thomas set up."

James felt a sickening lurch of recognition. Harold Winters—a respected businessman, faithful congregation member for 30 years, and current chairman of the finance committee. A man above reproach in the community, whose daughter had attended the retreat with them just days ago. "Eleanor, whatever justice needs to be served, this isn't the way. Taking matters into your own hands—"

"I didn't want to," she interrupted, genuine grief breaking through her determined façade. "For 15 years, I prayed for institutional justice and for the church to purify itself from within. I gathered evidence, raised careful questions, and tried to work through the proper channels." The letter opener trembled slightly in her grip. "But they protected each other. Used their positions, their respectability, and their selective application of Scripture to silence any questioning."

"And now?" Detective Collins asked, her tone professional but not unsympathetic.

Eleanor seemed to come to a decision, her posture straightening with renewed purpose. "Now, the evidence speaks for itself." She gestured toward the document case. "Everything is there—organized, cross-referenced, and witnessed when possible. I'm not delusional, detective. I know my role now is to ensure this documentation reaches the proper authorities without being intercepted or altered."

The tension in the chapel eased fractionally as both James and Detective Collins recognized that Eleanor's immediate intentions were not violent, regardless of whatever plans she might have harbored earlier.

"What about Harold Winters?" James asked. "And Gregory's attorney? You said they refused to confess."

A shadow crossed Eleanor's face. "I visited Harold this morning before coming here. Left him a detailed account of his involvement, with copies of financial records bearing his signature. Told him he had until noon today to contact the authorities and confess voluntarily." She checked her watch. "That deadline has passed. The information has been automatically sent to the FBI and the district attorney's office."

"You set that up as a failsafe," Detective Collins realized. "Insurance that the evidence would be released, even if something happened to you."

"Precisely. I may be an old woman, detective, but I've worked with computers since they first appeared in the church's office. Scheduled emails are not difficult to arrange."

Despite the seriousness of the situation, James felt a reluctant admiration for Eleanor's meticulous planning and her resolve to uncover the whole truth regardless of the personal cost. "And now?" he asked softly.

Eleanor looked at the letter opener in her hand as if seeing it for the first time, then placed it carefully on a nearby pew. "Now, I step aside and let justice take its course." Her voice carried both resignation and satisfaction. "My role in this story is complete."

Detective Collins stepped forward cautiously, securing the letter opener before directly addressing Eleanor. "Ms. Simmons, I need to take you into custody for questioning about your involvement in recent events, including potential conspiracy charges related to Michael Chen's removal from the retreat."

Eleanor accepted her fate with dignified composure. "I understand. I directed Martin to take the boy when I realized Thomas had identified him as a threat. I believed it was the only way to protect him until the documentation could be secured and released." She then met James' gaze directly. "I never intended for Michael to be traumatized or for his mother to suffer. My goal was to keep him safe for a brief time until Thomas could be exposed."

"Your intentions will be noted," the detective assured her, proceeding with a formal arrest while treating the elderly woman with proper respect.

As Eleanor was being escorted from the chapel, she paused beside James. "Revelation 2:2," she whispered. "'I know your deeds, your hard work and your perseverance. I know that you cannot tolerate wicked people, that you have tested those who claim to be apostles but are not, and have found them false.'"

The verse—a commendation from Christ to the church at Ephesus for their discernment against false leaders—served as Eleanor's final justification for her years of vigilant documentation and her refusal to accept deception within the church she loved. "The church isn't buildings or leaders or programs," she continued, her voice carrying the weight of decades of faithful service. "It's the people of God committed to truth, to justice, to genuine faith expressed through love. Don't let them forget that, James."

With that charge ringing in his ears, James watched as Detective Collins led a handcuffed Eleanor from the chapel. The elderly church secretary walked with the dignified bearing of someone who had completed a long, solitary mission and was prepared to accept whatever consequences followed. The document case—Eleanor's meticulous record of 15 years of conspiracy, cover-up, and corruption—remained in the storage space beneath the platform, awaiting official processing. James stood before it, overwhelmed by the magnitude of what had been revealed and what still remained to be disclosed when those records were thoroughly examined.

His phone rang, jolting him from his contemplation. The screen displayed Rebecca's number from the hotel. "Rebecca? Is everything alright?"

"James," her voice came through tense but controlled. "Harold Winters just surrendered himself at the police station. It's all over the local news. He's confessing to involvement in the youth center cover-up, saying he can't live with the deception any longer."

Eleanor's ultimatum had worked, pushing at least one conspirator toward voluntary confession rather than public exposure.

"And there's more," Rebecca continued. "FBI agents have taken Michael's statement about the blueprints he found. They've been gentle and professional. He's handling it all remarkably well." She paused. "He asked me something I wasn't sure how to answer. He wanted to know if our church would still exist after this."

The question struck at the core of what James had been grappling with since the conspiracy began to fall apart. What was left of their faith community after such deep betrayal by its leaders? What could be saved, rebuilt, and redeemed?

"Tell him," James said after a thoughtful pause, "that the church existed before these leaders and will exist after them. That the truth, however painful, makes room for something more genuine to grow. That God is present in the revealing as much as He was absent in the hiding."

"I'll tell him. Promise. And James? Eleanor... did you find her?"

"Yes. She's being taken into custody, but she's safe. She had been documenting everything all along, gathering evidence against Thomas and the others involved."

"Wow. All this time," Rebecca marveled. "Working silently and patiently while being overlooked by everyone."

"Not everyone," James corrected, thinking of Ethan, Martin, and the careful network Eleanor had built to protect her evidence and ultimately, to shield Michael. "She found allies when needed, including your son, whose innocent discovery finally brought everything to light."

After ending the call, James stood alone in the chapel, surrounded by colored light from the stained-glass windows, facing the pulpit where Scriptures had been proclaimed—both honestly and manipulatively—over the years. The document case waited to be officially processed, its contents soon to reveal the full extent of the conspiracy that had corrupted First Community Church from within.

The biblical concept of revelation—'apokalypsis' in Greek, literally meaning "an unveiling" or "uncovering"—had never seemed more fitting. What had been hidden was now being revealed. What had been whispered in the darkness was being proclaimed in the light. The divine whispers that guided Eleanor's patient documentation, Michael's innocent discovery, and even James' own involvement in unraveling the conspiracy had ultimately proven stronger than the human efforts to suppress them.

As he turned to leave the chapel, James noticed something he had overlooked before: a small plaque on the wall beside the door, installed years before his arrival as pastor. It bore a single verse, Proverbs 12:19:

"Truthful lips endure forever, but a lying tongue lasts only a moment."

Fifteen years of deception, manipulation, and corrupt leadership finally yielded to the persistent truth. The monumental revelation was complete—painful but necessary, though it left the community to face the judgment that followed and, ultimately, the chance for true restoration.

Chapter 11: Redemption's Edge

Three days after Eleanor's arrest, James stood before the congregation at First Community Church, facing a sea of shell-shocked faces. The sanctuary, usually alive with the soft hum of pre-service chatter, was now held in an unyielding grip of tense silence. News of the conspiracy had spread across national media, turning their humble community church into the center of a sensational story involving murder, cover-up... and religious hypocrisy.

"I want to begin," James said, his voice steady despite his inner turmoil, "by acknowledging the full truth of what has happened. This church's leadership, entrusted with spiritual authority, betrayed that trust in profound ways. They concealed a murder, misused donated funds, and threatened the life of an innocent child to protect their deception. There is no minimizing or excusing these actions."

Heads nodded throughout the congregation, with some bowed in grief and others raised in anger or defiance. James recognized the full range of reactions—denial, rage, bargaining, grief—the stages of traumatic loss unfolding across the community he had been called to shepherd.

"What happened cannot be undone," he continued. "But how we respond as a faith community—with truth, repentance, and the determination to create safeguards against future abuses of power—that choice belongs to us." He paused, surveying those before him. Some familiar longtime members sat beside newcomers drawn by the media coverage. Rebecca and Michael occupied a pew near the front, the boy leaning against his mother, resilient yet still processing his role in the unfolding drama. Ethan was notably absent, still cooperating with investigators following his release on bail for his role in Michael's removal from the retreat. "The road ahead will not be easy," he acknowledged. "Trust has been broken. Faith has been shaken. The very concept of church authority has been called into question. These wounds will not heal overnight, nor should they. Genuine healing requires unflinching honesty about the injury, not premature declarations that everything is fine."

At the back of the sanctuary, Detective Collins stood quietly observing. She had come, not in an official capacity, but as someone personally invested in the aftermath. Her presence reminded James of the complexity of the moment— simultaneously a criminal justice matter, a crisis of faith, and a community trauma requiring delicate navigation.

"I believe," James continued, "that today embodies what Scripture calls 'Kairos time'—a pivotal moment when decisions and actions carry extraordinary significance. We stand at redemption's edge, where the path forward requires both justice and mercy, both accountability and grace."

A small commotion at the sanctuary's entrance drew attention. Harold Winters, recently released on bail pending trial for his role in the financial aspects of the conspiracy, entered hesitantly. His appearance—unshaven, disheveled, with his usual impeccable business attire replaced by casual clothing—reflected his dramatic fall from pillar of the community to acknowledged conspirator. Murmurs spread through the congregation as he made his way to an empty seat near the back, shoulders hunched under the weight of public judgment. James noted the mixed reactions—some recoiled in disgust, others watched with wary curiosity, and a few showed glimmers of compassion for a fallen neighbor.

"Many have asked me," James said, deliberately drawing attention back to his message, "how we rebuild after such betrayal. My answer begins with a foundational truth: the church was never meant to be built on human personalities or leaders, but on Christ Himself. When we elevate humans to pedestals—whether in church, politics, or the community at large—we create the conditions for precisely this kind of tragedy."

Harold's unexpected presence had created a perfect, though unplanned, illustration of James' next point. "Part of our path forward involves understanding the difference between accountability and abandonment. Those responsible for wrongdoing must face justice—both legal and communal. But Christian redemption means we never write anyone off as beyond the reach of grace, no matter how grievous their failures."

As he continued outlining principles for the congregation's healing journey, James was struck by the profound irony of the situation. By betraying the church through conspiracy and deception, Thomas and his collaborators inadvertently opened the door for genuine renewal—a removal of false piety and institutional self-protection that had hidden deeper corruption.

"Effective immediately, we will implement new governance structures," he promised. "Financial transparency, distributed authority, limits on pastoral power, and independent accountability mechanisms. But these procedural changes, while necessary, are not enough without spiritual transformation—a renewed commitment to truth-telling regardless of the cost, to questioning authority properly, to valuing justice above institutional reputation."

As he concluded his address, James invited anyone who wished to speak to come forward—an unprecedented move in their traditional service structure, but one he felt essential for beginning genuine healing. "This pulpit has too often been a place of one-way communication," he explained. "Today, we open the floor to your voices, your grief, your questions, your anger, your hopes. The path to redemption begins with truth, both spoken and heard."

What followed was one of the most extraordinary services in the church's history. One by one, members approached the microphone James had placed in front of the pulpit. Some spoke through tears. Others expressed determination to rebuild with greater integrity. A few directed pointed questions at Harold, who sat receiving their judgment with his head bowed.

Rebecca eventually rose, walking to the microphone with quiet dignity that commanded attention. Michael stayed in his seat, watching his mother with solemn eyes. "My family came to this church seeking healing after my husband's death," she began. "We found community, purpose, and what I believed was authentic faith. When Michael was taken, that foundation was shattered." She paused, gathering her thoughts. "I've been struggling with how to reconcile the genuine love I experienced here with the corruption that existed alongside it." The congregation hung on her every word, a collective breath held as this most devastated member shared her perspective. "What I've realized," she continued, "is that both were real. The corruption was real. The love was also real. The prayers that sustained my son and me after David's death came from sincere hearts, even if some church leaders were living double lives. The meals delivered during our grief, the Sunday School teachers who nurtured Michael's faith, the friendships that carried us— those weren't invalidated by what certain leaders did."

James observed the reactions around the sanctuary to her words: nodding, crying, and trying to process the complexity she articulated so clearly.

"I don't know yet what my family's relationship with this church will be going forward," Rebecca admitted. "But I do know that abandoning faith entirely would mean Thomas Webb gets the final word in my and my son's spiritual journey, and I refuse to give him that power."

Her statement, delivered without dramatic flourishing yet carrying profound weight, seemed to unlock something in the room. Perhaps it was a shared permission to reveal both grief and hope, both judgment and the possibility of reconciliation.

As others continued sharing, James watched Detective Collins quietly slip out of the sanctuary. He made a mental note to talk to her later, curious about her reaction to this unusual service and the traumatized faith community taking its hesitant first steps toward healing.

****

The meeting room at the county justice center bore little resemblance to the warm sanctuary James had left just hours earlier. Stark fluorescent lighting, institutional furniture, and the presence of FBI agents created an atmosphere of clinical officialdom as they gathered for what was described as a "critical update" on the investigation.

Detective Collins greeted James as he entered, her professional demeanor slightly softened by their shared experiences. "Thank you for coming, Pastor Miller. We wanted you to be present for this briefing, given your involvement in the case and your ongoing support of those affected."

James nodded, noting Rebecca's presence across the room, speaking quietly with an FBI victim advocate. "Any word on Eleanor?" he asked. The elderly church secretary's status had been his ongoing concern since her arrest.

"That's part of what we'll be discussing. Please, have a seat."

As the meeting began, FBI Special Agent Townsend took the lead, outlining the developments in the investigation that had expanded far beyond the original discovery at the youth center. "Based on Eleanor Simmons' documentation," he explained, "we've identified financial transactions connecting Thomas Webb to multiple entities beyond First Community Church. These include charitable foundations, real estate holdings, and offshore accounts that appear designed to obscure the flow of funds." He displayed a complex diagram on the wall screen, showing the intricate web of connections that Eleanor had painstakingly mapped over the course of 15 years. "Simply put, what began as concealment of a single criminal act evolved into a sophisticated system of financial manipulation. Thomas Webb effectively created a parallel structure alongside legitimate church operations, siphoning donations, manipulating property transactions, and ensuring silence through strategic payments disguised as consulting fees or administrative services."

"Like the phantom payments using Eleanor's name," James observed, remembering her distress at this discovery.

"Exactly," Agent Townsend confirmed. "Ms. Simmons first suspected misconduct when she accidentally discovered financial records showing payments to her that she'd never received. That discovery 15 years ago began her documentation project."

Rebecca leaned forward, her expression troubled. "But how does this connect to Michael's kidnapping? To what he discovered in the blueprints?"

Detective Collins took over the explanation. "As the youth center renovation neared, Lawrence Peterson's legal challenge to his father's donation created a perfect storm. The construction would disturb the site where the bodies were buried, potentially exposing the original crime. Simultaneously, the legal proceedings risked revealing the financial irregularities surrounding the donation."

"And Michael innocently stumbled into the middle of this," James concluded grimly.

"Yes. When he found those blueprints and began asking questions about the discrepancies, Thomas Webb recognized an existential threat to everything he had built." Detective Collins' expression softened slightly. "What we didn't fully understand until reviewing Eleanor's documents was that Michael wasn't the first to notice the inconsistencies." She nodded to an assistant, who displayed a new image on the screen—a photograph of a teenage boy standing proudly next to a church youth group banner, his smile carefree and innocent. "Jacob Mercer. Seventeen years old, reported missing six years ago during a church youth service project. The case was investigated as a possible runaway and eventually went cold when no leads surfaced."

James stared at the image, cold realization dawning. "He was part of our youth group. The police interviewed me when he disappeared. I was told he'd left a note suggesting he planned to leave town."

"A note that Thomas Webb 'discovered' and turned over to investigators," Agent Townsend confirmed. "Eleanor's records suggest Jacob had been asking questions about financial discrepancies he noticed while volunteering in the church office. She believes Thomas eliminated him when those questions became too pointed."

The revelation hit hard. One concealed murder may have led to another, with corruption spreading like cancer through the institution Thomas had vowed to protect.

"We've reopened the Mercer case," Detective Collins said. "Forensic teams are examining additional areas of the church property based on Eleanor's documentation. There's a possibility that—" she paused, glancing at Rebecca before continuing, "that Michael was not the first child Thomas targeted to protect his secrets."

Rebecca paled but kept her composure. "You're saying my son could have been killed if Martin and Ethan hadn't intervened?"

"The evidence suggests that possibility," Agent Townsend acknowledged soberly. "Which brings us to our current situation and the purpose of this meeting." He distributed sealed envelopes to everyone present. "These contain details of a credible threat against key witnesses in this case, particularly Michael Chen and Eleanor Simmons. We believe Richard Peterson's brother, Robert, who was not previously on our radar, has hired professional assets to eliminate those who would testify against his family."

James opened his envelope, scanning its contents with an increasing alarm. "Robert Peterson? I don't remember that name being linked to the church."

"He wouldn't be," Agent Townsend explained. "Robert Peterson has lived overseas for decades, managing the family's international interests. He's also, according to Interpol, connected to various illegal enterprises that launder money through legitimate Peterson family businesses."

"And now, he's targeting witnesses," James concluded, the implications chilling. "Including an eight-year-old boy."

"We've already enhanced security for all identified targets," Detective Collins assured them. "Ms. Chen and Michael are being moved to a federal safe house tonight. We're here to discuss your situation, Pastor Miller."

"My situation?" James echoed, surprised.

"Your sermon this morning was livestreamed," Agent Townsend explained. "Your public stance against the conspiracy and your support for the witnesses put you on the threat assessment list. We're recommending temporary relocation until Robert Peterson is apprehended."

James absorbed this, his mind racing through the implications. "What about Eleanor? She's the linchpin of the entire case. Her documentation, her testimony—"

"Ms. Simmons is being transferred to federal custody for her protection," Detective Collins confirmed. "Which presents a logistical challenge. The transfer creates a window of vulnerability we're working to minimize."

As they discussed security protocols and arrangements for the days ahead, James found himself pondering the growing repercussions of the truth being uncovered. What had started as one child's innocent discovery had unraveled a decades-old conspiracy that revealed multiple crimes and now risked potentially deadly retaliation.

The meeting concluded with somber efficiency, with each participant assigned protective details and provided with emergency protocols.

As they prepared to depart for their respective safe locations, Rebecca approached James. "I never imagined that Michael finding those blueprints would lead to all this," she said quietly.

"Neither did Thomas," James replied. "He underestimated a child's perception and an elderly secretary's determination. Pride has always preceded the fall of the powerful."

Rebecca managed a slight smile despite the circumstances. "Speaking of Eleanor. She asked to see Michael before being transferred. The FBI approved a brief visit tomorrow morning at a secure location." She hesitated. "She asked if you would be present as well."

"Of course. I'd like to see her, too."

As they parted ways, James found himself reflecting on the strange journey that had brought them to this point. A pastor with a detective's background. A church secretary with a whistleblower's courage. A mother with a warrior's determination. And a child whose innocent questions had toppled a corrupt empire—each playing their part in a drama that transcended individual intention, moving relentlessly toward a greater purpose.

****

The safe house where Eleanor was meeting with Michael looked like a regular suburban home. Its plain exterior concealed high-level security systems and federal agents both inside and patrolling outside. James arrived with his security team, finding Rebecca and Michael already seated in the living room with two agents keeping a subtle watch nearby.

Michael smiled happily when he saw James, some of the wariness leaving his young face. "Pastor James! Are you hiding from the bad men, too?"

'The uncomplicated directness of children,' James reflected, *'can cut through pretense like nothing else.'*

"Something like that," he acknowledged with a smile. "How are you doing, Michael?"

The boy thought about the question carefully. "Mom says we're like David hiding from King Saul in the caves. The bad people want to hurt us because they're afraid of the truth, but God is protecting us."

James glanced at Rebecca, impressed by her ability to frame their situation within a biblical narrative that made sense to her young son while recognizing the real danger they faced. "That's a very good comparison," he agreed. "David had to hide for a while, but eventually, he was safe and became a king, just as God had promised."

Their conversation was interrupted by Eleanor's arrival, escorted by federal marshals who stayed professionally attentive to their elderly charge. Despite her situation—three days in custody and facing uncertain legal repercussions for her involvement in Michael's removal from the retreat—she carried herself with notable dignity. Her white hair was neatly styled, her clothes simple yet pressed, and her gaze was clear and direct as she entered the room. "Michael," she said warmly, her face softening at the sight of the boy. "Thank you for agreeing to see me."

Michael studied her with the frank curiosity of childhood. "Mom says you tried to protect me from Mr. Webb. That you knew he was doing bad things for a very long time."

Eleanor nodded, taking a seat across from him with the careful movements of age. "I did. I wish I could have stopped him sooner, before you became involved. But sometimes, even adults don't know the right things to do right away."

"Like David in the cave," Michael suggested, building on the analogy his mother had provided. "He had to wait for the right time to be king."

A smile touched Eleanor's lips. "Exactly like that. Very perceptive, young man."

One of the federal marshals cleared his throat gently. "Ms. Simmons, I need to remind you that this meeting is being recorded and that you should avoid discussing specifics of the case."

Eleanor acknowledged this with a dignified nod before turning her attention back to Michael. "I wanted to talk to you about two things, dear. First, I apologize that my efforts to protect you caused fear and separation from your mother. That was never my intention."

"It's okay," he replied with the simple forgiveness children can sometimes offer more readily than adults. "Mr. Grayson let me keep Shelly, and Mr. Parker made sure I could write to my mom."

"And the second thing is to thank you. Your bravery in noticing what adults had overlooked or ignored helped bring the truth to light. Sometimes, God uses the most unexpected people as His instruments of justice."

"Mom says the same thing: that God used me even though I'm just a kid. Like Samuel in the temple, hearing God's voice when the grown-ups couldn't."

Eleanor's eyes shimmered with unshed tears. "Your mother is very wise." She looked at Rebecca with evident respect before turning to James. "And you, Pastor Miller. I owe you an apology as well. I should have trusted you with what I knew earlier."

James shook his head. "You had 15 years of evidence that church leadership couldn't be trusted, Eleanor. Your caution was understandable."

"Perhaps," she conceded. "But in my effort to document everything perfectly before stepping forward, I may have caused additional harm. The Mercer boy—" She paused, looking at Michael and clearly deciding that this topic was inappropriate in his presence.

One of the marshals checked his watch, then approached. "Ms. Simmons, we need to prepare for transport in five minutes."

Eleanor nodded her understanding, then turned back to Michael. "May I ask you something? When you found those blueprints and noticed they didn't match the actual building, what made you pay attention to that detail?"

Michael thought for a moment. "I like buildings," he explained simply. "Dad used to draw houses. He taught me how to read blueprints before he died. He said you should always check if things are built the way they're supposed to be."

The poignancy of this connection to his deceased father visibly touched everyone in the room. Rebecca reached out to stroke her son's hair, pride and sorrow blending on her face.

"Your father would be very proud of you," Eleanor told him softly. "You did exactly what he taught you. You noticed when something wasn't built the way it was supposed to be."

The marshal approached again, more insistently. "It's time, Ms. Simmons."

Eleanor rose with dignity, looking once more at Michael. "Thank you for seeing me, young man. Whatever happens from here, please know that your courage has made a big difference in many lives."

As she turned to leave, escorted by the marshals, James stood as well. "I'll walk you out, Eleanor." The marshals exchanged glances before nodding their permission. James accompanied Eleanor to the foyer, where they could speak briefly beyond Michael's hearing.

"The federal prosecutor has offered me a deal," she told him quietly. "Immunity in return for full testimony against all remaining conspirators. Apparently, my age and lack of prior criminal record make me a sympathetic witness rather than an appealing defendant."

"That's good news," James said, genuinely relieved.

"Perhaps. Though I'm ready to face whatever consequences arise. My focus now is on the church—on the congregation traumatized by these revelations."

"We're finding our way forward," he assured her. "Your documentation, as painful as its contents are, provides a foundation of truth upon which to rebuild."

Eleanor studied him with the penetrating gaze that had observed so much over her decades of service. "And you, James? Will you remain as pastor through this rebuilding?"

The question addressed his private struggles, the doubt that had haunted him since the conspiracy started unraveling. "I don't know," he admitted honestly. "I've been questioning whether the congregation needs a completely fresh start, untainted by association with previous leadership."

"If I may offer a perspective," Eleanor said thoughtfully. "The congregation doesn't need to be abandoned now, no matter how noble your intentions may be. They need a shepherd who understands both their trauma and their potential for healing—someone who has walked through the fire with them rather than someone who arrives after the crisis has passed."

Her words resonated with something James had been feeling but hadn't fully articulated. Before he could respond, however, a commotion erupted outside—raised voices, running footsteps, and the squeal of tires on the pavement. One of the marshals burst back in from outside, hand on his weapon. "Security breach! Vehicle approaching at a high speed, not responding to commands!"

Everything unfolded with disorienting speed after that. Agents rushed into the living room, guiding Rebecca and Michael toward a back exit. Others took defensive stances, weapons ready.

James was pulled aside by a marshal who moved him away from the windows while simultaneously calling for backup. "What's happening?" he demanded, instinctively heading toward Eleanor, who seemed forgotten amid the chaos.

"Stay back, sir!" the marshal barked.

Through the front window, James glimpsed a black SUV that had broken through the outer security perimeter and was now speeding toward the house. Agents outside had taken cover, weapons aimed at the vehicle.

"Multiple armed subjects," someone reported over the radio. "At least three, possibly four."

Eleanor moved with surprising speed for her age, gripping James' arm. "The Peterson family is more desperate than we expected," she said, her voice steady despite the situation. "They're not just eliminating witnesses one by one; they're trying a direct assault on many."

Before James could respond, the unmistakable sound of gunfire erupted outside. Sharp cracks were followed by the heavier report of shotguns. The marshal beside them cursed and spoke urgently into his radio. "They've engaged our perimeter team. All units respond. Package is moving to extraction point Alpha."

"Package?" James questioned.

"Michael Chen," the marshal clarified tersely. "Primary witness protection priority."

Another burst of gunfire, closer now, was followed by the sound of breaking glass somewhere at the rear of the house. Eleanor's grip on James' arm tightened. "They're trying to breach from multiple points," she observed with remarkable calm. "Classic tactical approach when the target's location within a structure is unknown."

James stared at her, momentarily distracted from the danger by this unexpected display of tactical knowledge. Eleanor caught his expression and managed to form a tight smile. "My late husband was military intelligence," she explained. I absorbed more than most realized."

Their conversation was cut short as a marshal physically pulled them toward a hallway. "This way! Now! We need to get you to the safe room."

As they moved through the house, James caught a glimpse of Rebecca and Michael being hurried out a rear door toward an armored vehicle. Relief washed over him at seeing them safely evacuated, quickly replaced by renewed fear as more gunfire erupted, now seeming to come from all directions.

"The extraction team is taking fire!" someone shouted over the radio. "Alternative route required!"

They reached what looked like an ordinary closet. The marshal pushed aside hanging clothes, revealing a reinforced door with a keypad. He entered a code, then urged them inside as the sound of breaking glass and splintering wood echoed through the house.

"They've breached the front entrance," he reported into his radio, following James and Eleanor into what proved to be a small, windowless room with concrete walls, emergency supplies, and communications equipment. "Package Two and Elder secured in panic room."

"Package Two?" James questioned as the heavy door sealed behind them.

"You," the marshal explained tersely, checking the monitoring screens that displayed various views of the house's interior and exterior. "High-value witness due to your involvement in exposing the conspiracy."

"And 'Elder'?" James asked, though he had already guessed.

"Me," Eleanor confirmed, taking a seat on a small bench with the dignity of a queen on her throne despite the chaos surrounding them. "Apparently, my age has become my identifier in security protocols."

Despite the serious situation, James had a fleeting urge to laugh at the absurdity of code names and security jargon used for a pastor and an elderly church secretary. The impulse faded quickly as the monitors revealed armed men moving through the house, methodically checking each room. "How many attackers?" he asked the marshal, who was dividing his attention between the monitors and his radio communications.

"At least five. Professional equipment and tactics. The response team is three minutes out."

On one monitor, James watched as Rebecca and Michael reached the armored vehicle, with agents forming a protective shield around them. They were almost to safety when a figure appeared from behind a hedgerow, weapon raised. "Look out!" he shouted uselessly at the screen, helpless to warn them.

A split second before the attacker could fire, one of the protective agents spotted the threat and pivoted, placing himself directly in the line of fire while simultaneously pushing Rebecca and Michael toward the vehicle. The agent fell as shots rang out, but his sacrifice bought the critical seconds needed for the others to get Rebecca and Michael into the armored transport.

"Agent down!" the marshal reported into his radio. "Extraction vehicle departing with primary package. Hostiles still on premises."

On the monitors, they watched the armored vehicle speed away, chased by gunfire that pinged ineffectively off its reinforced exterior. James exhaled a breath he hadn't realized he was holding, grateful for Rebecca and Michael's escape while praying for the agent who had made it possible.

"They'll concentrate on us now," Eleanor said calmly. "Once they realize their primary target has escaped."

As if confirming her assessment, the monitors showed the attackers regrouping and communicating through hand signals before spreading out to search the rest of the house. One approached the closet that concealed the panic room entrance, examining it carefully.

"Will they find us?" James asked quietly.

The marshal checked his weapon. "The room is designed to be undetectable without specialized equipment. But if they're as professional as they appear, they may be prepared for that contingency."

"How long until backup arrives?"

"Two minutes," the marshal replied, though his tone suggested those might be two very long minutes.

Eleanor kept watching the monitors with impressive calm, her hands folded in her lap as if she were waiting for a church service to start rather than possibly fighting for her life soon.

"You don't seem afraid," James mentioned, moving to sit beside her on the bench.

"Oh, I'm terrified," she corrected him with surprising candor. "But fear serves no useful purpose right now, so I choose not to indulge it." She looked at him with a hint of a smile. "Plus, I've had 15 years to prepare for the possibility that exposing this conspiracy might cost me my life. I made peace with that long ago."

On the monitors, they watched as the leader of the attackers examined the closet more thoroughly, running his hands along the edges of the wall in a manner suggesting he suspected something beyond.

"They know," the marshal said grimly, positioning himself protectively in front of James and Eleanor. "Standard procedure is to stay silent unless directly breached. Response team ETA is 90 seconds."

The attacker on the other side of the door produced what appeared to be a specialized electronic device, running it slowly across the wall. Its screen must have confirmed his suspicions, as he signaled to his companions, who took up different positions in front of and on the sides of the closet.

"They have detection equipment," the marshal reported into his radio. "Panic room location compromised. Expedite response."

James watched with a surreal sense of detachment as the attackers prepared what looked like breaching charges meant to break into their hideout. The concrete walls could withstand most firearms, but specialized explosives might create an entry point.

"If they breach," the marshal instructed quietly, "move to the far corner, behind the supply cabinet. I'll engage any hostiles that enter."

Eleanor nodded, her calm acceptance a striking contrast to the chaos happening around them. "Whatever happens, James, remember that truth wins in the end. Even if some who stood for it don't survive to witness that victory."

Her words carried such genuine dignity and unwavering conviction that James felt humbled beside her. Here was faith reduced to its core—not the performative piety Thomas Webb had perfected, not institutional power disguised as spiritual authority, but the quiet certainty of someone who had aligned herself with the truth regardless of personal cost.

On the monitors, they could see the attackers attaching their equipment to the wall concealing the panic room door. The marshal tensed, his weapon ready, preparing for the breach that seemed inevitable. Then, suddenly, the attackers froze, hands moving to communication devices in their ears. Their body language shifted from offensive to defensive as they exchanged urgent signals before beginning a rapid retreat from the house.

"The response team has arrived," the marshal announced with evident relief. "The hostiles are withdrawing."

Indeed, the monitors showed tactical vehicles surrounding the house, with heavily armed federal agents deploying in a coordinated response that clearly outmatched the retreating attackers. Gunfire erupted again, but now it was the Peterson mercenaries on the defensive, attempting to reach their vehicles as federal agents closed in from multiple directions.

"Two hostiles down," the marshal reported, watching the monitors. "Three attempting to flee northbound in a black SUV."

Within minutes, the situation had completely changed. The marshal received confirmation that the perimeter was secure, Rebecca and Michael had reached a secondary safe location, and medical aid was being rendered to the wounded agent whose sacrifice had secured their escape.

When the panic room door finally opened, they stepped out to find the house secured by federal agents. The attack had been thwarted, though signs of violence remained in broken windows, splintered doorframes, and bullet holes in the walls.

"Three suspects in custody, two wounded, none killed," a senior agent reported. "The remaining two escaped the immediate area, but roadblocks are already in place. It's only a matter of time."

"And Robert Peterson?" Eleanor asked, once again displaying her comprehensive grasp of the situation's dynamics.

"Interpol has located him attempting to board a private flight from Zurich to a non-extradition country," the agent replied. "He's being detained for questioning based on financial evidence your documentation provided, Ms. Simmons."

As they were escorted to a secure vehicle for transport to another location, James reflected on how narrowly tragedy had been avoided—and at what cost. An agent was wounded, perhaps critically. The peaceful suburb had transformed into a battlefield. Rebecca and Michael were forced to flee once again, their trauma compounded.

Yet alongside these sobering realities, he recognized something else at work: the unstoppable march toward justice that Eleanor had maintained faith in throughout her years of meticulous documentation. The powerful Peterson family, with all their wealth and connections, had failed to silence the truth. Their desperate final move had only sped up their exposure and downfall.

"It's almost over," Eleanor said quietly as they drove away from the compromised safe house. "Not the legal proceedings—those will continue for years. But the active danger, the immediate threat to Michael and the other witnesses."

"Thanks to your foresight," James acknowledged. "Your documentation provided the leverage for federal involvement, international cooperation, and the full apparatus of justice that even the Petersons couldn't overcome."

Eleanor gazed out the window, her expression pensive. "I was just one part of a larger process. Martin Grayson protected evidence for years before involving me. Ethan recognized corruption and acted when the time was right. You combined your pastoral and investigative skills to uncover the truth." She smiled slightly. "And an eight-year-old boy noticed when blueprints didn't match reality, asking the innocent questions adults had learned to suppress."

As they drove toward an undisclosed secure location, James reflected on the fragile line of redemption they had all traversed—that thin boundary between justice and vengeance, between truth's uncovering and truth's weaponization, between accountability and destruction. They had collectively walked that line, sometimes stumbling, sometimes unsure of their footing, yet ultimately finding a path that balanced both justice and mercy.

The conspiracy that started with hiding one man's murder grew over 15 years, corrupting church leaders, risking more victims, and eventually leading to an armed attack on witnesses. But it did not succeed. Truth, although delayed, threatened, and requiring great sacrifice to protect, ultimately came out on top.

Truth delayed is not truth denied.

In this, James recognized the deeper spiritual reality beneath the criminal investigation and legal proceedings—the fundamental conviction expressed in Scripture that light ultimately exposes what darkness hides, that truth ultimately wins against deception, no matter how strong its defenders may be.

They had all lived by this principle, not as mere abstract theology but through costly personal experiences. And while the wounds were real—affecting individuals, the congregation, and faith itself—the possibility of true healing could now start, based on truth that was finally revealed and acknowledged.

The vehicle carrying them turned onto a highway leading away from the city, away from First Community Church with its fractured congregation and painful revelations, away from the youth center where bodies had been hidden beneath biblical quotes about truth and integrity.

They were heading toward their own uncertainties—legal battles, rebuilding their congregation, and personal recovery—yet James felt a strange sense of peace beneath the chaos. They had reached the edge of redemption and, instead of falling into the abyss that had claimed Thomas Webb, had found solid ground on the side of truth, regardless of the cost or what lay ahead.

Chapter 12: Amazing Grace

Six months after the armed attack on the safe house, First Community Church held a service unlike any in its long history. The sanctuary, recently reopened after extensive renovations that intentionally transformed the space, was filled with a congregation deeply affected by the events that had taken place. The elevated platform and imposing pulpit, which had physically separated the clergy from the congregation, were gone. In their place stood a simple wooden table at floor level, among the circular arrangement of pews that now encouraged worshippers to see each other rather than focus solely on leadership at the front.

James Miller moved through the gathering, greeting members with handshakes and embraces, noticing the mix of familiar faces and newcomers attracted by the church's difficult but ultimately redemptive journey. The criminal cases against the remaining members of the conspiracy had drawn ongoing media coverage, but the congregation had slowly reclaimed its story, turning a tale of corruption into one of renewal.

"Pastor James!" called a voice that instantly made his heart smile. Michael Chen moved through the crowd of worshippers, with Rebecca close behind him. The boy had grown taller in these months, his face losing some of its childlike roundness, though his eyes kept their perceptive glow.

"Michael! Are you ready for your special role today?"

The boy nodded solemnly. "I practiced my reading all week. Mom helped me with the hard words."

Rebecca approached, her smile showing how much she had healed and transformed. "He's been rehearsing morning and night. I think the entire neighborhood has heard Psalm 40 by now."

James chuckled, noting how Rebecca had changed as well—a new confidence in her bearing, a hard-won wisdom in her eyes. The crucible of Michael's kidnapping, the revelation of church corruption, and the subsequent danger they had faced had forged something remarkable in this once-quiet widow. She now served on the newly established Ethics and Transparency Committee, bringing her professional skills and personal experience to the critical work of rebuilding church governance.

"Have you heard from Eleanor today?" Rebecca asked, her tone softening at the mention of the elderly church secretary who had become an unexpected ally and friend.

"She'll be here," James confirmed. "The federal marshals are bringing her directly from the courthouse. Her final testimony in the Peterson case concluded yesterday."

The comprehensive prosecution of the Peterson family became one of the most significant criminal cases in the state's history, expanding beyond the original murder and cover-up to include financial crimes, witness intimidation, and the armed assault that nearly claimed multiple lives. Throughout the proceedings, Eleanor Simmons served as the prosecution's key witness, her meticulous documentation providing the framework upon which multiple charges were built.

"Everyone's been asking about her," Rebecca said. "The congregation wants to express their gratitude personally."

James nodded, understanding the profound shift in perspective that had occurred. Eleanor, once the overlooked church secretary, had become a symbol of courageous truth-telling—an example of faith expressed through persistent pursuit of justice rather than institutional loyalty.

As the time for the service neared, James headed to the small preparation room that had replaced the traditional pastor's study. The redesign was purposeful, part of the physical reimagining of sacred space that mirrored the congregation's spiritual rebuilding. He found Ethan there, nervously adjusting his tie. "Second thoughts?" James asked softly.

Ethan looked up, his expression conflicted. "Not exactly. Just wondering if I deserve to be part of this. After everything that happened." In the months following the conspiracy's exposure, he faced legal consequences for his role in Michael's removal from the retreat. Though he was ultimately granted probation in recognition of his protective intentions, he resigned from his position as Youth Pastor, uncertain of his future in ministry.

"You acted to protect a child when you recognized the danger Thomas posed," James reminded him. "That took courage and moral clarity, even if your methods were problematic."

"I should have found another way," Ethan insisted, the regret still evident in his voice. "Should have trusted the authorities sooner."

"Perhaps," James acknowledged. "But today isn't about perfect decisions; it's about grace amidst our imperfections. About community healing that includes everyone touched by these events."

Ethan nodded, taking a steady breath as the sounds of worshippers gathering filtered in from the sanctuary. "Eleanor arrives today?"

"Any minute. Her testimony has concluded, though the trials will continue for months."

"She's an amazing woman," Ethan said with genuine admiration. "Fifteen years of patience while being completely underestimated by everyone around her. I only managed two years of investigation before acting impulsively."

"Different callings," James suggested. "Eleanor was called to document for the long term. You were called to intervene in the immediate crisis. Both were necessary in their own way."

A knock at the door interrupted their conversation. An usher appeared, his expression a mix of excitement and reverence. "She's here, Pastor Miller. With Martin Grayson, too."

James and Ethan exchanged surprised glances before following the usher into the sanctuary. Near the entrance, Eleanor Simmons stood, supported by a cane but otherwise looking remarkably vigorous for a woman who had endured months of high-pressure testimony and legal proceedings. Beside her, Martin Grayson stood with a solemn, weathered face. His powerful frame, slightly diminished by his time in protective custody, still conveyed strength, and his eyes were clear and alert.

A spontaneous ripple of recognition spread through the congregation as Eleanor slowly made her way down the center aisle, nodding respectfully to everyone. The symbolic importance of her presence—the church secretary whose hidden courage had ultimately uncovered corruption that professional investigators overlooked—created a strong sense of respect.

Martin followed with more hesitation, clearly uncomfortable with the attention but determined to be part of this moment of community reconciliation. Although he was initially charged for his role in Michael's removal from the retreat, he was also granted leniency due to his protective intentions. The investigation uncovered his complex role over 15 years—officially hired to monitor Peter Sanderson, but gradually becoming a secret ally in Eleanor's efforts to document, safeguarding evidence he believed might someday be needed.

James met them halfway down the aisle, gently embracing Eleanor before firmly shaking Martin's hand. "We didn't expect you today," he said to the caretaker.

"Eleanor insisted," Martin replied gruffly. "Said healing happens in community, not isolation."

"And she's right. Your presence matters, Martin. You were part of this story from the start. First, as an unwitting participant in the cover-up, then as someone who chose truth when the moment of decision came."

As they moved toward the front, James saw that the sanctuary was filled to capacity. Beyond the regular congregation, there were journalists, community members, and others attracted by the church's public effort to confront corruption within its leadership while refusing to abandon faith itself. The service was advertised as a "Restoration Sunday"— not claiming complete healing but recognizing significant progress toward wholeness for a fractured community.

When everyone was seated, with Eleanor, Martin, Rebecca, and Michael in the front row, James moved to the simple wooden table that replaced the pulpit. Behind him hung a new cross, crafted from reclaimed wood taken from the youth center during its extensive renovation—a deliberate symbol of redemption rising from the site like a phoenix.

"We gather today," James began, his voice carrying easily in the attentive silence, "not to declare our journey complete, but to mark how far we've come from the darkness into which our church had fallen. Six months ago, we uncovered the heartbreaking truth that trusted leaders had hidden serious crimes, prioritized institutional protection over truth, and used Scripture to maintain their lies." He paused, allowing the weight of this acknowledgment to settle among them. "That revelation came through unexpected messengers: a child who noticed architectural discrepancies, an elderly secretary who documented patterns over years, and a caretaker and youth pastor who chose to protect the vulnerable over loyalty to corrupt authority. Their courage forced us to confront uncomfortable truths not just about individuals who had betrayed trust, but about church structures that enabled and protected that betrayal."

Heads nodded throughout the congregation, with many eyes filling with tears at this forthright acknowledgment of institutional failure.

"Today, we acknowledge both how far we've come and how much farther we need to go. We've restructured governance, established strong accountability systems, and distributed authority instead of hoarding it. We've reimagined this physical space to reflect our theological dedication to community rather than hierarchy. But more importantly, we've started the more challenging work of spiritual rebuilding— learning to question authority appropriately, to value truth over comfort, and to understand that genuine faith requires transparency instead of fear-driven secrecy." He then gestured toward Michael, who rose and approached the table with the somber dignity children often bring to important tasks. James stepped aside as the boy opened a Bible nearly half his size.

"I'll be reading Psalm 40," Michael announced confidently. "Verses one through three." The congregation listened with immersed attention as his clear voice filled the sanctuary:

"I waited patiently for the Lord; He turned to me and heard my cry. He lifted me out of the slimy pit, out of the mud and mire; He set my feet on a rock and gave me a firm place to stand. He put a new song in my mouth, a hymn of praise to our God. Many will see and fear the Lord and put their trust in Him."

As Michael returned to his seat, visibly pleased with his flawless delivery, James recognized the deep relevance of the passage: its imagery of rescue from a pit, of establishing firm footing after instability, of replacing old lamentations with new songs. The congregation had, indeed, been lifted from a pit of deception, was finding solid ground after the earthquake of betrayal, and was learning to sing new songs of genuine faith after the old hymns had been corrupted by hypocrisy.

"Today," James continued, "we welcome several individuals whose journeys have been especially important in our community's recovery. I've asked Eleanor Simmons to share her reflections on her experience as someone who saw corruption firsthand while working patiently toward uncovering the truth."

Eleanor rose with deliberate dignity, making her way to the table with measured steps that betrayed her age but not her spirit. When she turned to face the congregation, her clear gaze conveyed the serene authority of someone who had remained faithful to the truth through decades of patient waiting. "For 27 years," she began without preamble, "I served as secretary to this church. I answered phones, prepared bulletins, maintained records, and was generally treated as a piece of furniture in meetings where important decisions were made. It was precisely this invisibility that allowed me to witness what others missed."

The congregation listened in respectful silence as she recounted the beginning of her suspicions 15 years earlier, her gradual accumulation of evidence, and her careful efforts to work within proper channels before eventually forming her own network of allies.

"I tell you this not to portray myself as heroic," she clarified, "but to show how God often works through those whom society considers the least significant. The elderly secretary, who was overlooked and underestimated, became the keeper of truths that powerful men were desperate to hide." She paused, her gaze deliberately moving around the sanctuary. "My documentation has now helped secure justice through legal systems. But the greater restoration is what I see happening in this congregation—the willingness to acknowledge institutional failure, to implement real accountability, and to recognize that faith communities must embody the transparency they preach rather than the secrecy they condemn in others."

When Eleanor returned to her seat, Rebecca stepped forward next. Her testimony centered on her experience as a mother whose child was endangered by church corruption, yet she found her way back to the faith community instead of abandoning it entirely. "There were moments," she admitted honestly, "when I questioned whether any church could be trusted after what happened to my son. Whether faith itself was worth saving if it could be so completely twisted by its supposed guardians." She described her spiritual journey through anger, disillusionment, and cautious reengagement. "What ultimately convinced me to stay was seeing how this congregation refused easy answers or quick fixes. You acknowledged the full extent of the betrayal, made real changes rather than superficial ones, and created a space for honest questions instead of demanding unwavering loyalty."

One by one, the others shared their perspectives. Martin spoke hesitantly about his growing awareness of the deception he was hired to uphold; Ethan acknowledged both his bravery in protecting Michael and his regret over the methods that caused additional trauma; and Peter [Christopher Scott] described his burden of maintaining a constructed identity while knowing the truth remained buried.

As the service continued with music, prayer, and communion shared in a circle rather than flowing from leadership to passive participants, James observed the visible symbol of a community slowly healing. Not through denying wounds but through honest acknowledgment. Not through forgetting but through remembering differently. Not through hurried declarations of restoration but through patient engagement with the difficult work of rebuilding trust.

After the formal service ended, the congregation gathered for a shared meal in the rebuilt fellowship hall. The space buzzed with conversations, tentative laughter, and organic interactions as people processed trauma together rather than alone.

James stood beside Eleanor, who observed the gathering with evident satisfaction. "When I began documenting Thomas' activities 15 years ago," she said quietly, "I never imagined this outcome."

"What did you imagine?" James asked, curious about her long-term vision during those years of solitary vigilance.

"Justice. Exposure of the truth. Accountability for those responsible." She gestured toward the lively community around them. "But this—genuine renewal born from painful revelation—this surpasses what I dared to hope for."

James nodded, understanding exactly what she meant. The congregation's journey had gone beyond simple legal results, becoming something deeper: a community changed by facing its darkest secrets instead of hiding them. "There's something I've been meaning to ask you. Something that's puzzled me since the investigation began to unfold."

Eleanor's eyes twinkled with unexpected mischief. "Whether an elderly church secretary could really maintain such comprehensive documentation without assistance?"

"Something like that. Your records were remarkably thorough, Eleanor. Professional investigators were astonished by their detail and organization."

She smiled mysteriously. "Of course, I had help. Not just Martin and eventually Ethan, though they were vital allies. But something more." She patted the worn Bible she always carried. "Proverbs 15:3 – 'The eyes of the Lord are everywhere, keeping watch on the wicked and the good.'"

"Divine assistance?" James asked, uncertain of her meaning.

"Call it that if you wish. I simply found that when one aligns oneself with truth, remarkable resources become available. Conversations overheard at precisely the right moment. Documents accidentally left visible. Technology malfunctioning in ways that preserved rather than deleted evidence." Her expression grew thoughtful. "Too many 'coincidences' to be mere chance."

Before James could probe further, Michael appeared beside them, his plate piled impossibly high with desserts. "Pastor James," he said with a mouthful of cookie, "my mom says I can join the new youth group if you think I'm old enough."

James smiled, delighted by this evidence of the boy's resilience and Rebecca's renewed trust in church programs. "I think that would be wonderful, Michael. The new Youth Director is planning activities that include children your age."

The new youth ministry, like everything else in the church, had been rebuilt from the ground up—with improved safety measures, transparent leadership, and age-appropriate opportunities for children to ask questions rather than just receive information.

"Cool!" Michael replied excitedly before turning to Eleanor with the innocent curiosity of childhood. "Miss Eleanor, my mom says you're like Esther in the Bible—that God put you in the church office so you could help when bad things happen, just like Esther helped her people."

Eleanor's face softened at this comparison. "Your mother is very kind, Michael. But remember that Esther had help from her cousin Mordecai and many others. Just as I received help from unexpected sources."

As Michael hurried away to join his friends, Eleanor's gaze followed him with clear affection. "Such a remarkable child," she murmured. "To go through what he did and come out not just unharmed but somehow changed by it is a blessing."

"Children often display surprising resilience," James replied. "Especially when adults around them acknowledge the truth rather than conceal it and offer genuine support instead of false reassurance."

"Something churches could learn from more often," she agreed.

Their conversation was interrupted by the approach of several congregation members eager to speak with Eleanor, whose semi-celebrity status as the key witness in the ongoing Peterson prosecution had transformed her from an overlooked secretary to a respected truth-teller. James excused himself, continuing to circulate through the gathering, noting with satisfaction the natural communities forming and reforming: grief groups finding solidarity in shared processing, governance communities discussing transparency mechanisms, and youths engaging with elders in ways previously discouraged by age-segregated programming.

Near the exit, James ran into Detective Collins, who had attended the service quietly and was now getting ready to leave. Their professional relationship had evolved into a cautious friendship as the investigation went on, mutual respect building through their shared dedication to the truth, despite approaching it from different angles.

"Remarkable transformation," she commented, gesturing toward the vibrant community behind them. "Most institutions close ranks when corruption is exposed. Deny, minimize, and scapegoat individuals while protecting systems."

"We tried that approach for 15 years," James admitted regretfully. "It almost destroyed us. But only by facing the full truth, no matter how painful, could real healing begin."

Detective Collins nodded thoughtfully. "I've seen many criminal investigations in religious contexts. Usually, the institution survives by distancing itself from 'bad actors' while leaving underlying patterns untouched." She studied the gathering with a professional assessment. "What's happening here is fundamentally different."

"We had extraordinary examples: Eleanor's persistence in documenting, Michael's innocent perception, Rebecca's refusal to accept comfortable lies, even Martin and Ethan choosing to protect the vulnerable over loyalty to corrupt authority." He smiled slightly. "And a detective who approached her investigation with both professional thoroughness and personal investment."

She acknowledged the compliment with a small nod. "The case concludes with sentencing next month. Richard Peterson has already accepted a plea deal in exchange for testimony against his brother Robert. Lawrence Peterson's challenge to the property donation has been withdrawn. The financial web Thomas built is being systematically dismantled by forensic accountants."

The legal resolution, though important, felt somewhat secondary to the human and spiritual revival happening around them. James saw this shift in perspective as a sign of his own healing, moving from initially focusing on criminal justice outcomes to recognizing a deeper reconciliation that went beyond legal procedures. "Will you continue attending services?" he asked, noting that Detective Collins had been present occasionally during the reconstruction process.

She considered his question thoughtfully. "Perhaps. There's something compelling about a faith community that has faced its darkest hours yet chose transparency over concealment and accountability over protection of power." A smile softened her usually serious features. "Besides, I've developed unexpected connections here." She nodded toward where Eleanor sat surrounded by congregants, her usually reserved demeanor warmed by evident affection for those seeking her wisdom. The unlikely friendship between the methodical detective and the patient church secretary had unfolded gradually during the investigation—two women from different generations but sharing a strong commitment to truth, finding common ground in their pursuit of justice.

After Detective Collins left, James found a quiet moment to stand alone and observe the community. Six months earlier, this congregation faced an existential threat, not just from the criminal conspiracy uncovered among them, but from the crisis of faith that such betrayal by trusted leaders naturally caused. Yet here they were—wounded but healing, disillusioned but not broken, navigating the difficult line between naïve trust and cynical disengagement. The experience had changed them both individually and as a group, making them more aware of corruption's warning signs, more willing to question authority when appropriate, and more committed to living out the transparency they claimed to value.

James' personal journey mirrored that of the congregation. His detective background, which he had previously kept hidden while embracing his pastoral role, had become integrated rather than separate—his investigative instincts now seen as compatible with spiritual leadership rather than in conflict with it. This experience had transformed his view of ministry itself. It became less about giving answers and more about asking better questions, less about maintaining appearances and more about seeking truth wherever it might lead.

As the gathering gradually dispersed, Michael approached once more, this time accompanied by his mother. "Pastor James," the boy said earnestly, "I've been thinking about something important."

"What's that, Michael?"

"When bad things happen, like Mr. Webb hiding the truth and taking me away from my mom, does God already know it will turn out okay in the end? Or is He surprised like we are?"

The theological depth of the question momentarily stunned James. Here was the central mystery they had all been circling: the relationship between divine foreknowledge and human freedom, between providence and contingency, between God's sovereignty and evil's apparent power.

Rebecca gave her son an affectionate smile. "That's a question many theologians have debated for centuries, sweetheart."

"But what do you think, Pastor James?" he persisted, looking at James with genuine curiosity.

James thought carefully about his answer, knowing that this child deserved a thoughtful reply rather than a simple platitude. "I believe that God sees the complete picture in ways we cannot. He sees the beginning, middle, and end of our stories all at once. So, while evil remains truly evil, and human choices matter deeply, God is working through all circumstances—even the most painful—toward ultimate redemption."

Michael nodded, processing the response. "Like when I found those blueprints. It was scary, and bad things happened, but it also made the truth come out so that the church could get better."

"Exactly like that. What happened to you was wrong, truly wrong. Nothing justifies your kidnapping or the fear you experienced. Yet somehow, God worked through even those terrible events to bring about something good that wouldn't have happened otherwise."

The theological principle, though abstract in academic discussions, had become real through their lived experience: the mysterious process by which divine purpose includes even human evil without lessening its true wrongness or erasing the significance of human choice.

As Rebecca and Michael left, James stayed to help clean up, working with congregation members on simple yet meaningful tasks that tie big spiritual ideas to everyday community life. While stacking chairs with a new member who had joined specifically because of the church's public stance on transparency, James caught himself reflecting on Eleanor's cryptic comments about 'coincidences aligning in service of truth's revelation.'

He recalled the unlikely sequence that had led to the conspiracy's exposure: Michael's unusual interest in architecture inherited from his father, his presence at exactly the activities where blueprints might be visible; Eleanor's strategic cultivation of allies over 15 years; the timing of Lawrence Peterson's legal challenge with the youth center renovation; and even his own unique blend of detective experience and pastoral role. Any single element could be explained as a coincidence. However, together they hinted at something more deliberate—what Eleanor had subtly suggested was divine orchestration guiding ordinary human choices toward extraordinary outcomes.

As the day drew to a close and James finally headed home, he found himself drawn to the newly renovated youth center. The building had been completely reconstructed after the excavation confirmed both murders: the business rival killed by Richard Peterson 15 years ago, and the child victim discovered beneath the foundation, eventually identified as a local boy who had gone missing decades earlier, long before the Petersons acquired the property.

The dark history beneath the structure had been acknowledged rather than hidden during the reconstruction. A memorial garden took up part of the site, featuring a plaque that listed the victims and committed the church to "truth-telling as a sacred obligation." The building itself was redesigned with physical transparency as the main principle—windows everywhere, open sightlines, and no hidden spaces or rooms accessible only to authority figures.

As James stood, observing this tangible symbol of institutional transformation, he noticed a stunning sunset forming above the mountains to the west. The clouds were lit up in brilliant gold and crimson, stretching across the horizon— a natural display that poets and theologians have long seen as divine communication. In that moment of solitary reflection, he felt something more than intellectual agreement: a bone-deep certainty that the arduous journey of recent months was not random chaos, but a purposeful resolution, not arbitrary suffering, but a necessary revelation, not just coincidence, but a divinely guided unveiling.

The theological term "amazing grace" took on new meaning—not just unearned favor but astonishing orchestration, the mysterious intersection of human freedom and divine purpose that could turn even the darkest human evil into an opportunity for redemption. The whispers of the Divine that guided Eleanor's careful documentation, inspired Michael's innocent questioning, and supported the congregation through their darkest hour had ultimately proven more powerful than the human systems designed to silence them.

As James turned to leave, he noticed something that stopped him midstride. There, at the edge of the memorial garden, stood an elderly man he didn't recognize, gazing solemnly at the plaque bearing the victims' names. Something about his posture conveyed profound grief.

James approached carefully, thinking he might be a relative of one of the victims. "Good evening, sir. I'm Pastor James Miller. Is there something I can help you with?"

The man turned to face him, revealing a deeply lined face that spoke of long-carried sorrow. "Just paying my respects," he replied, his voice gravelly with age. "Been meaning to visit for some time."

"Did you know one of the victims?"

"In a manner of speaking. I've followed this case from the onset, though from a distance."

Something about his phrasing struck James as unusual. "The beginning, meaning 15 years ago? Or the recent investigation?"

The elderly man smiled faintly. "Much earlier than that, young man. Some secrets stay buried longer than others."

Before James could say another word, the man nodded politely and turned to leave, moving with surprising speed for his apparent age. As he walked away, James noticed something that sent a chill of recognition through him: a distinctive turtle-shaped keychain hanging from the man's pocket, identical to the one Michael had described losing during his abduction. "Excuse me," James called, suddenly alert. "Sir? Sir? May I ask where you got that keychain?"

But the elderly visitor had already disappeared around the corner of the building. James hurried after him, only to find the adjacent street empty in both directions. There was no sign of where the man might have gone.

Confused but not worried, James went back to the memorial garden, wondering if the encounter was important or just a strange coincidence. As the sunset disappeared into twilight, he said a last prayer at the spot where truth had been buried and then uncovered. He prayed for gratitude for partial justice, for healing cautiously started, and for a community changed by facing, not hiding, its darkest chapters.

The mysterious visitor, whether an ordinary community member or someone more symbolic, seemed like a fitting final note in a story where the line between everyday reality and divine intervention had repeatedly blurred—where human choices carried their full responsibility while also serving purposes beyond individual intent.

As James finally headed home, with the first stars appearing in the darkening sky, he carried with him the profound awareness that had developed through these months of crisis and restoration: that truth, no matter how long suppressed, eventually finds its voice; that light, no matter how deeply buried, ultimately breaks through; and that grace, genuinely remarkable in its unexpected ways, transforms even humanity's darkest failures into opportunities for true redemption.

The divine whispers that guided their journey— sometimes subtle like Eleanor's quest, sometimes obvious like

Michael's innocent questions, and sometimes challenging like Detective Collins' penetrating investigation—had ultimately proven more powerful than human efforts to silence them. And in that reality lay the congregation's true foundation for rebuilding. Not human personality or institutional prestige, but alignment with the truth that transcended both.

Behind him, the memorial garden served as a reminder of the costs of hiding and the importance of acknowledgment. In front of him, a future unfolded—not with perfect clarity but with genuine engagement with the messy, beautiful, painful process of building community based on truth rather than comfort or deception.

Amazing Grace in the whispers of the Divine, indeed. Not as easy forgiveness without accountability, but as the mysterious alchemy by which even the darkest human evil could be incorporated into a larger narrative of redemption... precisely because the truth had finally been spoken aloud rather than whispered in the darkness.

Reflective Finale

The journey through *Whispers of the Divine* offers profound insights into faith, community, and the human tendency to prioritize institutions over those they are meant to serve. As we conclude this exploration, several enlightening truths emerge from the darkness that briefly surrounded First Community Church:

❖ Religious institutions, despite their sacred purposes, remain fundamentally human creations. The story of First Community Church illustrates how easily power can corrupt, how readily financial considerations can supersede moral obligations, and how thoroughly self-preservation can overshadow a commitment to the truth. Thomas Webb's 15-year conspiracy reveals the uncomfortable reality that religious language and authority can be weaponized to silence questioning and maintain systems of manmade power.

❖ Yet paradoxically, this institutional failure paved the way for genuine renewal. Only by addressing the corruption at its core could the church community understand what true faith looks like beyond the comfort of hierarchical certainties. The fall of corrupt leadership structures created an opportunity for a more transparent, decentralized model of spiritual community, one focused on accountability rather than blind loyalty.

❖ Perhaps the most moving part of this story is how truth surfaced through those usually ignored or underestimated. Michael Chen, an eight-year-old boy with an innocent curiosity about architectural drawings, saw what powerful adults had intentionally hidden. Eleanor Simmons, the elderly church secretary treated as "furniture in the room," patiently documented patterns of corruption that professional investigators overlooked. Martin Grayson, the socially awkward caretaker, kept evidence that eventually became crucial for justice.

This pattern reflects a spiritual principle common in many religious traditions: that divine wisdom often manifests through unexpected channels, challenging our assumptions about who deserves attention and whose perspectives matter. The "whispers of the Divine" in this narrative came not through official pronouncements from the pulpit but through a child's questions, an elderly woman's meticulous record-keeping, and a caretaker's moral awakening.

Thomas Webb and his co-conspirators operated from a fundamental misunderstanding: that protecting faith required hiding the truth. They justified deception, financial manipulation, and even threats against an innocent child as necessary to preserve the church's mission and reputation. This reflects a serious theological mistake: the belief that God's work depends on humans managing reality through deception.

The spiritual journey of First Community Church shows that genuine faith thrives not in carefully maintained illusions but in courageous honesty. Rebecca Chen's evolution illustrates this truth. Her faith was not broken by institutional betrayal but rather transformed from a passive acceptance of authority to an active engagement with deeper spiritual principles. By refusing to give up faith entirely while also rejecting corrupt forms of it, she embodied the narrow path between cynical disengagement and naïve trust.

The transformation of the church provides a blueprint for institutional redemption that goes beyond religious settings. Their path forward did not start with reducing harm or blaming individuals to protect the systems, but with a firm recognition of the full scope of betrayal. The physical redesign of their sanctuary—replacing hierarchical architecture with circular seating, removing the elevated pulpit, and introducing transparency in the rebuilt youth center—demonstrated their commitment to structural change instead of just cosmetic improvements.

This approach sharply contrasts with how institutions usually handle exposing wrongdoing. Instead of protecting reputations at all costs, the congregation focused on truth rather than comfort, accountability instead of appearance, and real reform rather than quick fixes. Their experience shows that true healing, both personal and communal, involves facing the pain of honest reckoning rather than avoiding it.

Pastor James Miller's distinctive background—combining detective work with pastoral care—enabled him to navigate the tension between justice and mercy that often divides religious communities during crises. His method balanced accountability with forgiveness and stayed compassionate in the fight for justice. He showed how these seemingly opposed values actually depend on each other for authentic expression.

The legal proceedings against those involved in the conspiracy represented a necessary form of justice. Yet alongside these consequences, a process of community healing also emerged, recognizing human complexity. Harold Winters' voluntary confession and attendance at the Restoration Sunday service demonstrated this integration, facing legal accountability while also being embraced by the complicated, messy process of communal restoration.

Perhaps the most profound insight emerging from this narrative is that faith itself transcends the institutional structures created to nurture it. When Rebecca questioned whether their church would continue to exist after such devastating betrayal, James responded with wisdom that speaks to our contemporary context of declining institutional trust: "The church existed before these leaders and will exist after them." This view provides hope in a time when religious institutions across various traditions face struggles with relevance and legitimacy. It indicates that the core of faith communities—their ability to connect people to transcendent purpose, ethical principles, and a supportive community—can endure and even flourish amid radical change. What might not survive are specific forms of religious authority that focus on maintaining institutions at the expense of human well-being.

The conclusion of this journey hints at something beyond human control: what Eleanor cryptically called "too many coincidences to be mere chance." The intersection of Michael's architectural interest inherited from his father, Eleanor's careful cultivation of allies over 15 years, James's unique mix of investigative and pastoral skills, and many other "coincidences" suggests a mysterious force at work—one in which even human evil is woven into a larger story of redemption.

This perspective doesn't diminish the true wrongness of the conspiracy or the trauma it caused. Instead, it recognizes the paradox that healing often comes from wounds, that light is most visible in darkness, and that resurrection naturally follows crucifixion. The elderly visitor with the turtle keychain in the final scene embodies this mystery, hinting at connections beyond logical explanations.

As we conclude this exploration, we are not met with a clear resolution but with an invitation to embrace the complexity of faith in a broken world. The "whispers of the Divine" persist, speaking through unexpected messengers, calling us toward difficult truths, and guiding us through darkness instead of around it.

And in that journey—painful and uncertain, yet ultimately transformative—we learn that authentic faith doesn't depend on perfect institutions or unquestioning loyalty, but on the courage to align ourselves with the truth, no matter the cost, and trust that redemption comes after revelation.

The story of First Community Church becomes more than a cautionary tale about religious corruption. It presents a vision of hope that communities can confront their darkest failures and emerge not diminished but strengthened, not weakened but genuinely renewed. In this paradoxical journey from darkness to light, from whispers to proclamation, from devastating truth to amazing grace, we see the enduring power of faith that transcends human frailty while working through it toward goals of restoration and redemption.

20 Thought-Provoking Questions for Book Discussion Groups

1. Throughout the story, Pastor James Miller grapples with the dual roles of pastor and ex-detective. How does this internal conflict influence his response to the developing crisis, and what might it reveal about the balance between justice and mercy when confronting institutional corruption?

2. Eleanor Simmons spent 15 years documenting church corruption before the truth came to light. What does her patient vigilance reveal about power dynamics in religious institutions, especially regarding who is recognized versus who is ignored?

3. Thomas Webb justified his actions as "protecting God's work" and serving "the greater good." How does the story challenge or complicate the idea of sacrificing moral principles for institutional preservation?

4. Rebecca Chen faced a deep crisis of faith when she discovered the church's corruption. How does her spiritual path from trust to disillusionment to cautious reengagement reflect larger questions about faith enduring institutional betrayal?

5. Michael Chen's innocent discovery of architectural discrepancies acts as the catalyst for revealing decades of corruption. What might this imply about the role of childlike perception versus adult complicity in preserving systems of deception?

6. Detective Sarah Collins is haunted by trauma from a previous child abduction case, where her professional judgment failed. How does this past influence her approach to Michael's case, and what does her character arc say about redemption for those who feel responsible for others' suffering?

7. The physical change of the church building—shifting from hierarchical architecture to circular seating with leadership at ground level—reflects the community's spiritual transformation. What message does this redesign send about authentic religious communities?

8. When Eleanor states, "I was just one instrument in a larger process," she points to a divine orchestration beyond human planning. How does the narrative explore the tension between human agency and divine purpose in bringing justice?

9. The story shows both the failure of official systems (law enforcement, church leadership) and the success of unofficial networks (Eleanor's documentation, Martin and Ethan's intervention). What could this imply about institutional reform versus grassroots change?

10. Martin Grayson holds a morally blurred role: first hired to cover things up, but later working to safeguard Michael. How does his character challenge simple ideas of guilt and redemption?

11. The first youth center is built literally on buried crimes. How does this physical reality serve as a metaphor for institutional religion built on hidden corruption, and what does the eventual excavation symbolize spiritually?

12. The narrative showcases different types of courage: Eleanor's patient documentation, Michael's innocent questioning, Rebecca's maternal protection, and James' confrontation of church leadership. How do these various expressions of courage work together and complement each other?

13. When faced with evidence of corruption, different congregants respond with denial, anger, grief, or a commitment to rebuilding. How might these reactions reflect the stages of grief, and what does this imply about how a community processes trauma?

14. The Peterson family leverages wealth and influence to cover up crimes and silence witnesses. How does the story explore the connection between economic power and accountability, especially within religious settings?

15. The mysterious elderly visitor with the turtle keychain in the final chapter introduces an element of ambiguity. What purpose might this supernatural encounter serve in the story that's otherwise rooted in realistic human interactions?

16. Eleanor quotes Proverbs 15:3: "The eyes of the Lord are everywhere, keeping watch on the wicked and the good." How does this theological perspective serve as both comfort and challenge throughout the story?

17. The "restoration" of the congregation explicitly avoids claiming complete healing. What might this imply about genuine community renewal versus surface-level reconciliation after betrayal?

18. Both Thomas Webb and Eleanor Simmons selectively quote Scripture to justify their actions. How does the narrative address the potential for religious texts to be weaponized for opposing purposes, and what criteria does it suggest for authentic interpretation?

19. Michael questions whether God is surprised by events or already knows everything that will happen. How does the story explore the theological conflict between divine foreknowledge and human free will, particularly in relation to evil actions and their potential redemptive outcomes?

20. The phrase "whispers of the divine" seems to refer both to the quiet questioning that reveals truth and the subtle divine guidance working through seemingly random events. How does this dual meaning mirror the story's view of how God interacts with human affairs?

About the Author

Angela R. Edwards is the Chief Editorial Director of Pearly Gates Publishing, LLC (PGP) and Redemption's Story Publishing, LLC (RSP)— Award-winning International Hybrid Christian Publishing Houses located in the Central Savannah River Area of Georgia. In May 2018, PGP was honored as the 2018 Winner of Distinction for Publishing in South Houston, Texas, by the Better Business Bureau (BBB). From 2018 to the present, she has been the recipient of BBB's Gold Star Certificate for both entities, recognizing her exemplary service to the community.

Angela lives by *"My Words Have POWER!"* Since its inception in January 2015, PGP has been blessed with an ever-growing and diverse group of over 100 authors who have penned topics related to faith, love, abuse, bullying, Christian fiction, Bible study tools, marriage, and so much more. Their youngest author was two years old; their eldest is 83 at the time of this publication. To their credit and God's glory, PGP and RSP have collectively over 150 bestselling titles to date, including a literary work penned by Mr. Jimmy Merchant, formerly of the 1950s Doo-Wop group, "Frankie Lymon & The Teenagers," with their most recognizable music hit, *Why Do Fools Fall in Love.*

An affordable publishing option (in comparison to some of the larger, traditional publishing houses), PGP and RSP work one-on-one with authors, ensuring that financial hardship is not a discouraging aspect of the publishing process. For those desiring to share their God-inspired messages, both publishing houses provide unique services and support that many have said "left them feeling as if they were the only author" under each company's care.

The Holy Bible states that *"God loves a cheerful giver"* (2 Corinthians 9:7). To that end, PGP and RSP frequently host fantastic publishing giveaways. Throughout the past few years, new author contests have awarded authors collectively with $18,000.00 in services.

Angela is also a self-published author, producing works that utilize her writing skills, which date back to second grade, when she won awards for creative writing. She has since earned the title of #1 International Bestselling Author for titles including the *Divine Detours* Christian Romance fiction series, a ten-book teen series titled *Heritage Quest*, exploring the Fruit of the Spirit, and her tell-all abuse-survivor story titled *The Bathroom Was My Dungeon*.

In addition to the aforementioned, Angela is a domestic abuse survivor. Since first telling her abuse survivor story publicly, she has become a "Trumpet for Change." She is the Founder of the Battle-Scar Free Movement, Inc.—a 501(c)(3) nonprofit that provides resources to abuse victims and survivors as they transition to a life free from abuse. As part of her God-given mission, she provided abuse victims and survivors a free opportunity to anonymously share their testimonies in a seven-book series titled *God Says I am Battle-Scar Free*. Although the series is complete, Angela's mission to help individuals heal with the power of their words continues.

Assisting others with the healing process is paramount to her, which led her to volunteer for two years at the Star of Hope Mission in Houston, Texas, as their first-ever Domestic Violence Liaison.

Angela holds an A.A. degree in Business Administration from the University of Phoenix and is pursuing a B.S. degree in Psychology with a concentration in Christian Counseling from LeTourneau University. She is a woman of God, a wife, a mother, a grandmother of 23, and a trusted friend. Originally from New Jersey, she has since made Georgia her home and fully embraced the Southern culture.

Angela loves life and affirms daily: ***"NOT TODAY, SATAN! AND TOMORROW ISN'T LOOKING TOO GOOD, EITHER!"***